RONALD GEORGE

Elizabeth Franklin

A Witch's Tale

This novel is entirely a work of fiction. The names, characters and incidents portrayed in it are the work of the author's imagination. Any resemblance to actual persons, living or dead, events or localities is entirely coincidental.

This book and its characters portray the practice of witchcraft that for fictitious purposes have been exaggerated and may or may not resemble the actual practice itself.

First edition

This book was professionally typeset on Reedsy.
Find out more at reedsy.com

Contents

Acknowledgement

I would like to thank those that were instrumental in getting this book completed:

My parents for all of their love and support.

Patty Ringer for editing, research and development.

Michael Ringer, owner of Skill Capture Media, for graphic arts and illustrations/photography.

Steven Ringer for website development.

Model, Shelly D'Inferno, for her amazing photoshoots as Elizabeth Franklin.

Heather Gauthier, owner of Feisty Witches on Facebook.

Cheryl Trigones Riley, owner of Facebook page Wicca & Witchcraft for Beginners.

1

Introduction

"Elizabeth," she could feel her grandmother's voice inside her head call out as she opened her eyes. "Awake from the darkness dear child," her grandmother spoke once again.

"Grandmother?" Elizabeth acknowledged.

"Yes my young apprentice, it is I," she replied. "The time has come. A gateway will open to the other world on Hallows Eve."

"Are you certain?" Elizabeth asked.

"I have foreseen it," she answered. "Soon your spirit will escape from the hell from which it has been enslaved."

"How long has it been?" Elizabeth asked.

"Over 150 years," her grandmother answered.

"I see," she replied, with little regard. "And where will this gateway open?"

"In the Franklin mansion," her grandmother informed her.

"Home," Elizabeth answered with a sigh. "How fitting."

"Fools have their ways," she replied. "But in this case, it welcomes our needs."

"Do explain," Elizabeth demanded.

"I cannot explain it," her grandmother replied. "It is beyond our reasoning."

"Nothing is beyond reason," Elizabeth answered back through her mind.

"It is a dimension of which I know nothing," her grandmother admitted. "Only that a gateway will open."

"And through this gateway of which you know nothing you doom me to pass?" Elizabeth asked.

"Do you wish to remain in hell, or do what I bid you?" her grandmother asked angrily.

"I am in hell, because I did what you said," Elizabeth answered. "Or has 150 years played tricks on your mind and vanquished your memory?"

"I warned you there would be consequences!" her grandmother rebutted. "What you did was on your behalf and of your own doing. You were just careless and paid the price."

"Fine grandmother," Elizabeth conceded. "I will do as you say. If you are correct, then the witch of a Franklin will live once more."

"Perhaps," her grandmother said. "Don't be overconfident. It was always your weakness!"

"And lack of faith in me yours," Elizabeth returned.

"You still have much to prove for my faith to meet your expectations," her grandmother countered.

"Leave me," Elizabeth requested. "I will meditate."

"As you wish child," her grandmother agreed. "Just be prepared."

"I will be," Elizabeth assured her.

"Only your soul will be free," her grandmother continued. "You will not be of flesh and blood."

"We shall see," Elizabeth stated. "This dimension of which you know nothing could prove advantageous."

"Yes," her grandmother agreed. "But show no mercy. Whomever you encounter in the land of the living must die. They will be of no use to you and must not be made aware of who you are and from where you have come."

"Understood, grandmother," Elizabeth accepted.

"Then it is done," she said, content in the plan. "I will speak no more of this."

"Blessed be, grandmother," Elizabeth said, from darkened eyes that for the first time in a century and a half began to resonate the color of sapphire blue.

"Hell hath no boundaries!" she exclaimed, while electricity began to swirl through her opened eyes.

"Not for you," her grandmother agreed. "That is for certain."

2

HALLOWS EVE

"Embark not on this journey,
divination speaks clearly,
Heed the runes or pay you shall dearly."

"Did you get the beer?" Mike shouted out of the open passenger window, casually resting an arm across the black leather upholstered seat of his car, his voice competing against the rumble of the exhaust pipes that had suddenly awakened the sleepy night air.

"Of course," Tyler answered, walking over to Mike's jet black 1969 Chevelle and hearing the gravel of the stone road beneath his sneakers crunching with every step. "You're late," he said, reaching the passenger door.

"Yeah, my old man was giving me some shit before I left," Mike responded, resting his hand firmly across the ball of the four speed manual gear shift, shaking slightly in sync with the engine's growling roar.

It was an unusually warm night for this time of year in South Carolina. Especially Halloween night, when jeans and jackets are normally required. So warm, in fact, that it was reminiscent of a not too distant summer gone by. Whereas tonight, shorts and tank tops were the attire of choice. "I've been standing out here for like the last hour," Tyler complained, opening the car door and climbing in.

"What do you want me to say bro?" Mike asked, putting the car into gear and taking off slowly.

"Well, we do have these," Tyler replied, holding his cellphone in the air to demonstrate.

"Where are we going?" Mike asked, squinting his eyes into the pitch black darkness that even his headlights weren't helping much with.

"The stream," Tyler answered, motioning with a pointed finger. "Up ahead a bit. I stashed it there this afternoon. Should be good and cold."

"Chris got it for you?" Mike asked, glancing over at him while his car crept along slowly.

"Yep," Tyler answered.

"He's a good man, but if my daddy knew he was buyin' us beer he'd skin us both for asking him," Mike pointed out.

"Stop. This is it right here," Tyler said, as he peered through the windshield. "You're still wearing that?" he asked, noticing a shiny silver bracelet dangling from Mike's wrist as he opened the car door and caught a glimpse of it from the dim lit interior light. "Unbelievable."

"Just get the beer, alright?" Mike replied.

Mike knew what was on Tyler's mind. He didn't have to be reminded. The gamers' convention, THE gamer's convention, where the best in the world compete in Las Vegas for a winner takes all prize of a hundred grand, and he had held the title. He was ranked number one. All he had to do was pick the best partner, and the money was in the bag. Tyler was the obvious choice for a two player combat game that relied heavily on the buddy system. "Warlords and Wizards" was a game the two of them had mastered to perfection. They could anticipate each other's moves in their sleep. But when the time came, at the last minute, he had asked his girlfriend Jenny to partner with him instead.

Normally that would have driven a stake straight through the heart of their friendship, but Tyler took it in stride. Money, regardless of how much it amounts to, is just money. Friendships, on the other hand, are priceless. So instead, Tyler competed against him, frustrated and knowing none of them would win, except maybe Jenny. She would get the fame and glory in all the gamer magazines for being the partner of the world's number one ranked gamer. She wasn't even close to deserving that privilege.

"She will be there tonight," Mike confessed, as he grabbed the flashlight laying on the console and climbed out of the car. "So keep your mouth shut about the convention."

"Wait, why is she coming?" Tyler asked, jumping around the front of the car to meet up with him. "I didn't invite her."

"No, but Steve did," Mike said, clicking the flashlight on and proceeding through the thick weeds to the stream not too far away in the distance.

"Yeah, but…" Tyler began to say as he followed behind him, wanting to say something and deciding it was better not to. Jenny had broken up with Mike three months ago. Nobody saw that one coming, especially Mike. Even worse, she hooked up with Steve. That was like pouring piss on an open wound. He was one of them…a gamer… more like a brother actually. Mike took it well-enough but deep down inside, if you peeled back the layers of his thick skin, he was hurting.

"You didn't think Steve would bring her?" Mike stopped, noticing Tyler's silence and turning the flashlight onto his face.

"Actually, no," Tyler answered.

"Yeah, well guess again," Mike returned, hesitating momentarily to see if Tyler had anything else to say before giving up and returning the flashlights beam to the stream ahead that they were approaching.

Mike was the bigger of the two, not particularly tall but stocky and broad in the shoulders. He was proud of his physique that came from endless hours of working on the farm, hefting bales of hay and whatever else called upon his strength of youth to perform. It was all he knew since he could remember, and he wore it well.

Tyler, on the other hand, was more on the lean side. He wasn't skinny by any means, but he was no comparison to Mike. And Mike had the facial hair. A year ago, when he was seventeen and had a full beard, he could have easily passed for twenty-one.

"There," Tyler pointed, seeing the case of beer now completely submerged in the streams cold water.

"I got it," Mike said, handing the flashlight over to Tyler and pulling it up effortlessly.

"Anyway…" Tyler began, while the two of them made their way back to the car. "If Jenny is going to be there, why the hell are you wearing her bracelet? I mean, do you want to embarrass yourself or what?"

Mike thought about what Tyler had said as he trudged back through the weeds carrying the case of beer over his shoulder.

"I'm just saying," Tyler pushed, as they neared the car.

"I still love her," Mike finally admitted, grabbing the handle of his door and tossing the case into the backseat.

"What?!" Tyler exclaimed. "Are you crazy?"

"Probably," Mike agreed, reaching into his pocket for a pack of cigarettes.

"Dude, seriously," Tyler said, standing in front of him. "She never loved you in the first place. She played you like she played games."

"I don't believe that," Mike said, speaking with a cigarette between his lips as he tilted his head slightly to light it.

"Look, I didn't want to say this, but…" Tyler began.

"Then say it," Mike pressed, taking a drag and exhaling into the night air.

"You picked Jenny for your partner, alright," Tyler replied, feeling the phone in his back pocket vibrate. "And she wasn't ready. It should have been us."

"She was ready," Mike shot back, irritated and watching as Tyler retrieved his phone. "I just made some mistakes and it cost us." But that wasn't true and Mike knew it. He was defending Jenny at whatever cost. She was no way near ready to compete with him at such a high level. Love has its price.

"You lost because she sucked," Tyler replied, reading his text messages.

…where the fuck are you?

…we are here

…where's the game?

"What's this about anyway?" Mike asked, changing the subject. "This game I mean…what's the deal?"

"You'll find out," Tyler answered, as he typed the words…on our way, ten minutes…into his cell phone. "We gotta go."

After a little less than a ten minute drive along mostly dark lit roads, Mike pulled his car into the dirt covered driveway of an abandoned plantation mansion that had to be at least a hundred years old. There were three other cars already parked haphazardly along the overgrown weeds, and he could see Steve and Jenny, arms crossed against their chests and leaning up against a brand new red GT Mustang as his headlights hit them. Jenny was wearing black Converse shoes, denim jean shorts and a black t-shirt. Her long blonde hair was draped across her shoulders and partially covering the words, "I paused my game to be here" written across her t-shirt in bold white letters.

"Turn them off already!" she shouted, holding her hand up to block the blinding light.

He couldn't make out the other two cars, as they were parked further away and not in the direction of his headlights, but he knew who they were…Brandon Johnson and Phil Myers. A few summers ago, they all had worked together on his father's farm. It was only for a couple months, but in that short amount of time they had become good friends. Well, not as close friends as him and Tyler were. Mike had known Tyler since grade school. But they were good drinking buddies and excellent gamers. As he parked the car and silenced the rumbling engine, he could see them making their way through the thick weeds towards him. Brandon was tall and lanky, smoked cigarettes at about the same pace as Mike, and wore a tattooed sleeve on his left arm. One could argue that he didn't look like a gamer, but then what is a gamer supposed to look like? You're either good or you're not. Winning does not discriminate based on appearance.

Phil was almost a mirrored image of Brandon with the exception that Brandon's hair was down to his shoulders and Phil kept his short. And like Brandon, he wore a tattooed sleeve, only on the opposite arm. As they got closer, Mike could hear the sound of weeds pushing back against black engineer boots and blue jeans and could see the ember of a lit cigarette moving up and down through the black night, highlighted even more so as he turned off the headlights.

"Tell me you brought some beer bro," Brandon said, approaching the driver's side of Mike's car and hoping not to be disappointed.

Mike leaned over into the backseat and twisted a can from its plastic ring, handing it to Brandon, as he stuck his head through the open window.

"Dude, we've been waiting out here for almost an hour," he complained, taking the beer and cracking it open. "What up Tyler," he added with a nod.

"Hey Mike, hey Tyler," Phil said from behind Brandon and received a nod back from both of them.

"So what's this about?" Brandon asked, lowering his voice to a whisper. "And why is Jenny here?"

"I didn't invite her," Tyler jumped in.

Mike glanced over at her through the windshield. It was surreal to see her standing there as if nothing had ever happened between them. He wondered if she was thinking the same thing.

"It's cool man, don't worry about it," he answered. "I didn't think Steve would come without her anyway."

"So, we're playing a game, right?" Brandon exclaimed excitedly and stepped back from the car. "Let's get this party started!"

"Not just a game…THE game," Tyler stated, as he opened up the car door to climb out. Mike doing the same and grabbing the case of beer to place on the hood of the car.

"How's it going Mike?" Steve asked, walking over and extending out his hand.

"It's been awhile," Mike replied, as they shook hands.

Not that it wasn't an awkward situation for him, considering the girl he still loved was standing across from him. But he never blamed Steve. Steve had actually come to him asking for his permission to date her. It wasn't his permission to give, but that's what friends do. Well, that's at least what his friends do. And he appreciated that. True, it had been awhile since they saw each other last, but not because of Jenny. Steve had been studying nonstop for his entrance exam to State College to be a software engineer. Gaming software to be exact. He was the only one in the group that not only had amazing gaming skills, but also the brains to design them.

"Hope you're not rusty," Mike said with a grin.

"Never!" Steve replied.

"Hey Jenny," Mike said, feeling his knees wanting to buckle as their eyes met.

Jenny shuffled on her feet and smiled, trying her best not to give too much away. She was happy to see him again. More than happy actually, ecstatic would be a better way to describe it. But she didn't want to be too obvious in front of Steve.

"I'll take one of those beers," she said, realizing immediately that she came across colder than she meant to.

Mike grabbed one off the hood to hand to her, expecting more from the conversation, as Tyler gathered everyone around.

"Alright, listen up," he began. "The game we're about to play is a prototype. It's not licensed. It's not for sale on the market. It's never been played, and its state of the art virtual reality."

"Virtual reality?" Brandon asked. "You mean with headsets?"

"Exactly," Tyler answered.

"We played around with them at the convention this summer," Mike added. "It's supposed to be the next big thing in gaming."

"Yeah, but the technology needs years to develop," Phil joined in. "I mean, it's like in its infancy stage."

"Not exactly," Steve interjected. "I've seen software designs that are crazy sophisticated."

"So how did you get it?" Jenny asked.

"That's not important right now," Tyler replied. "What's important is that we are the first ones to test and play it."

"I'm in," Mike said.

"Yeah bro I'm in," Brandon said.

"I'm in," continued the rest in chorus.

"Alright, so I set everything up in this old house where we always game. Got gas for the generator," Tyler stated. "Only problem is…" he continued, as he looked over to Jenny. "I only have 5 headsets. I wasn't expecting six people."

Jenny looked down at her shoes feeling the sting of his words. She was an outsider now. That was painfully obvious.

"It's fine," Steve said, putting a hand on her shoulder knowing what she was thinking. "You can grab one as soon as someone games out."

"Shit, that won't be me bro," Brandon said.

"I ain't gamin out," Phil added.

"Uh huh, we'll see," Steve smirked.

"Okay, so we're ready?" Tyler shouted out.

They were all more than ready at this point. Three months had passed since the gamer's convention. It was the last time they had played together as a team before Mike and Jenny took the trip to Las Vegas to compete. As much as it seemed odd to see Jenny back, at the same time it felt normal. Mike pumped his fist into the air, full of adrenaline. "Let's do it!" he whooped.

"Dude, don't forget the beer," Brandon pointed to the hood of the car, noticing Mike leaving it abandoned.

3

THE GATEWAY

"Return Spirit to your realm alas,
Thru the Gateway your soul shall pass"

"This house gets creepier every time we come here," Jenny stated nervously, looking up at the second story windows every time a break in the foliage of the surrounding trees allowed a glimmer of moonlight to sneak by, following the lead of Tyler's flashlight.

"Last time we were here was before we broke up," Mike whispered to Jenny, walking in front of her.

"Yeah, you're right," Jenny turned her neck back to agree.

It was so quiet that the only sound was that of the overgrown brush crunching beneath their feet, or the jingle of someone's change shuffling in their pocket. You could see the dark shadows of vines stretching like veins, digging themselves into the structure as if they were alive and trying to consume it. The top windows were broken out, leaving only sharp edges of glass in the corners of the frames. The paint, or what was left of it, was peeled and blistered from countless years in the sun.

"Shh!" Tyler said, stopping at once. "Do you hear that?"

"What?" Jenny asked nervously, putting her hand on Tyler's shoulder for comfort and pressing closer. "I didn't hear anything."

"That! Listen!" Tyler whispered, as a scurrying sound came from behind the back door he was about to open.

"Someone's in there," Mike whispered, moving in front of Jenny next to Tyler and the door.

"What's going on?" Brandon asked from behind.

"Shh!" Mike and Tyler replied simultaneously, looking back with a finger to their lips.

"Alright, on three we open the door," Mike stated.

Tyler shook his head yes in reply. Holding his fingers out, Mike counted down and then shoved the door open quickly.

"Ahh!!" Jenny screamed, as something bolted through the door and bumped into her leg, almost knocking her over.

"What the fuck was that?!" Mike shouted, as Tyler aimed the flashlight towards Jenny's direction.

"Shit. It's just a raccoon," Steve let out a sigh of relief, as he caught the last glimpse of it running away and out of the flashlights beam.

"Jesus, that scared the shit out of me," Mike said.

"Alright, it's cool," Tyler said, turning the flashlight into the room to survey further. At one time it was probably a parlor. A place for the gentlemen of the time to hang out, smoke cigars, and talk politics. But now all that remained were a couple dilapidated sitting chairs and a busted piano leaning recklessly to one side of a missing support leg. Tyler had cleaned out most of the cobwebs, but spiders are busy creatures. Already, they had made new webs over the game console stand, game box, and screen, making them look as old as the furniture in the room they accompanied. Curtains from the time period draped both of the boarded up front windows of the room, adding a smell of must and rotting fabric to the layers of dust on the floor. At one point, years ago, they had walked through the entire house, but there wasn't much to see. Most of the chandeliers had been removed and stolen. Faded wallpapers in every room were falling down in a rolled position, as if they were trying to come off of the walls themselves. In some rooms, the floorboards were so rotten you would surely fall through if you tried to step on them. The Parlor (as they called it) was the safest room in the house to game and party. And there was no reason to worry about the police. There was nothing in either direction on this road for miles and miles.

"Looks fine," Mike determined, after Tyler had made a few passes across the room with his flashlight.

"Yeah, let's get some power in here," Tyler agreed.

Brandon grabbed the flashlight from Tyler and headed back outside with Phil right behind him. The generator was placed inconspicuously behind a tree, not too far from the house. A long yellow extension cord was left plugged in, completely covered by the thistle and weeds and leading to a small hole in the foundation wall to a multi-plug inside.

"When's the last time we fired this thing up?" Brandon asked Phil, as he removed a blue plastic tarp covering it. "Here, hold this," he added, handing Phil the flashlight.

"I don't know…what… a couple months I guess?" Phil answered, shining the light on the generator that was beginning to show signs of neglect. Rust corroded the tips of the spark plugs, and the bright red paint of the engine housing and frame was raised up and flaking off.

"Yeah, well it's a piece of shit, so I hope it starts," Brandon said, as he took the cap off and grabbed a can of gasoline sitting next to it.

"It'll start," Phil replied, struggling while holding the flashlight in one hand and trying to light a cigarette at the same time.

"What are you trying to do, kill us?!" Brandon exclaimed, grabbing the still not lit cigarette from Phil's mouth and tossing it to the ground. "I'm pouring gas you idiot!" he noted, with a quick slap of his hand to Phil's head.

"So seriously dude, where did you get this game?" Steve asked Tyler, while they all stood in the dark waiting for the generator to kick on.

"I told you, it's not important," Tyler answered.

"I mean, so what…some dude just walked up to you, handed you a prototype that's probably worth a fortune, and said 'Here enjoy?'" Steve carried on.

"Something like that," Tyler shot back.

Steve wasn't buying it. He knew what went into the software for these types of games. They were extremely expensive to produce and cutting edge technology for gamers. Nobody would just hand over a prototype that wasn't copyrighted. Something was fishy.

"Since when do you give a shit about bootlegged games?" Tyler asked, sensing Steve's discourse. "We've played a lot of them."

"But this is different man," Steve said. "If this game is what you say it is…"

"Alright, knock it off," Mike jumped in. "We haven't even played it yet. Let's see what it's about."

"Power!" Brandon cheered, as the generator sputtered to life.

"Let the games begin dude," Phil replied smiling.

"Yeah, but I need a beer," Brandon said, trudging back through the weeds to the house.

4

THE GAME

"Pardon from death you must beseech,
Dark shadows of evil are well within reach,
Go back whence you came,
This place you must leave,
Lest your souls be taken on this Hallow's Eve"

Jenny squatted down to the floor, wiping away the dust with her hand and cringing. "You seriously need to get some chairs in here Tyler," Jenny said, as the lamp sitting alone on the floor next to her lit up. "So tired of sitting on the floor. It's disgusting!"

"It's a virtual game, so more than likely we're standing anyway," Tyler replied, as he reached behind the console stand to drag out a large cardboard box.

Virtual reality games were new, but Jenny remembered one in particular at the convention that had impressed her. She had never seen anything like it. "Did you guys check out that rollercoaster simulation at the convention?" she asked, with the thought still fresh in her head. "Omg, it was so realistic, like you were actually riding it."

"Didn't see that one," Mike returned, raising a beer can to his lips, taking a long gulp and then wiping his mouth with the back of his hand to continue. "But there was a ride I went on when I was a kid at Pixel studios, where you stood up and there was a huge 360 degree panoramic screen all the way around you. And they had these bars in front of you to hold onto. So anyway, it was a roller coaster simulator also, and everyone was grabbing those bars and hanging on for dear life.

"It fucks with your head," Steve joined in, raising his own beer in agreeance. "Same principle as virtual reality."

"So, that's it?" Brandon asked, returning from outside with Phil and grabbing a beer from the floor, noticing a small cartridge in Tyler's hand.

"Yep," Tyler replied, as he placed the cartridge on top of the game box.

"Damn dude these things look expensive," Phil exclaimed, reaching into the open box to retrieve a headset to examine.

"Pass them around to everyone," Tyler said. "I'm going to load the game."

"I'll get the light," Jenny said, stooping down to switch off the small shade-less lamp on the floor.

"So it should come up on the screen first and then…" Steve began, as they all huddled around.

"Here it is," Tyler interrupted, as the words TIME TO DIE appeared across the 65-inch screen. They were all in white capital letters and shimmered slightly, as blood rolled down each letter one at a time until completely covered.

"Well, at least we know it's not a roller-coaster game," Brandon said sarcastically.

"Probably a combat game," Mike interjected.

"Strange there's no music or more graphics," Steve commented.

"It's a prototype," Tyler replied. "They'll add that stuff later."

A moment later the blood-red words disappeared from the screen and were replaced with simulated typing, one letter appearing at a time and making clicking sounds similar to what you hear when you text. They began with…*select ….number of players….* followed by a screen that showed a glowing green keyboard with numbers from 1 to 10. Tyler wasn't sure what to do, but for the sake of trying he reached for the screen and pressed the number 5. *A.c.c.e.p.t.e.d.* typed across the screen.

"Touchscreen, impressive," Steve commented.

C.h.o.o.s.e…y.o.u.r…z.o.n.e typed next.

"I don't understand," Tyler said. "What does it mean 'choose your zone'?"

"I don't know," Steve admitted.

"Like a battle zone?" Jenny asked, perplexed.

"Yeah, but where are the options?" Brandon asked.

C.h.o.o.s.e…y.o.u.r…z.o.n.e typed the words again, as if the game was becoming impatient.

"What zone?!" everyone asked in unison.

"I guess there are no instructions, right?" Phil asked.

"No," Tyler replied, still staring at the words on the screen.

"Wait a minute," Mike said. "It's a touchscreen, right? So, press on the words."

Tyler did as Mike suggested and instantly the screen changed with the words…*Boundary Zone Options*…at the top of the screen and a simulated keyboard with the words…*type your dimensions*… underneath.

"I get it," Steve concluded. "It's virtual reality, so it has to set the playing field. We need the size of this room."

"No tape measure," Tyler returned.

"So, guess," Mike said, turning around to survey. "This room's what… 30 feet by 30 feet?"

"Probably something like that," Phil agreed.

"Type in 30 X 30," Mike suggested.

Tyler punched in the number 30 x 30 on the keyboard and waited. After a short pause, the words...*t.o.o...s.m.a.l.l...f.o.r...m.o.r.t.a.l...c.o.m.b.a.t...* flashed across the screen..

"Dude, I told you it was a combat game!" Mike said with satisfaction.

...*d.o...yo.u...w.i.s.h...t.o...p.r.o.c.e.e.d?* typed across the screen.

"I don't know," Jenny interjected. "This is a little creepy."

"Just do it," Brandon told Tyler. "Worst case scenario we get our asses kicked."

...*yes...* Tyler typed into the keyboard.

...*your opponents...*typed across the screen before switching to a new one showing their first of five opponents.

His name was Zeltar. It did not list height or body weight or any characteristics like most games did. Only a picture. He was at least 6'5" and incredibly muscular with gray skin. His face looked pretty much like your typical demon with vampire-like teeth. Only he had yellow eyes and claws for toes. And he was holding a battle axe twice its normal size.

"Shit, you can have him," Tyler said looking over to Mike.

"Thanks, Buddy," Mike returned sarcastically.

...*Madelin...* flashed the name of the next opponent, with her image.

"Typical female flesh-eating zombie," acknowledged Jenny. "I can take her, no problem."

...*Ghostess...*came the following opponent. Her name was a creative play on words, as she was dressed as a blonde female restaurant hostess, wearing a black skirt and blouse uniform opened at the top to show her cleavage.

"What the hell?" Brandon questioned, looking at her picture and not understanding why she would be an opponent. And then suddenly the image changed, showing her with a ghost-like, almost see through appearance. Her face had turned into a completely bare skull with only her blue eyes intact. And she was holding a razor-sharp butcher knife.

"How do you kill a ghost, man?" Brandon asked.

"You have to wait until they appear in human form," Mike answered with experience from previous games fighting ghosts. "You gotta be quick."

...*Chain*... was the next opponent. Easy enough to figure out by his name, this guy was dressed in a black executioner's hood like the ones they put over the head of a person to be executed. It had no holes for eyes, nose, or mouth and was wrapped tightly around his neck with thick barbed wire. He was bare chested, exposing a huge muscular upper torso and wore black wrestlers shorts. His thighs were as thick as most men's waists, and he was holding a chain that was so long that at least 10 feet of it laid on the ground beneath his feet.

"Any takers on him?" Phil asked.

"Chains are easy to beat if you know what you're doing," Steve replied. "Like in Dragonworld. I crushed at that game."

...*Mirror...What you see is what you get*...

"Huh? I don't get it," Tyler asked confused.

There was no image of the opponent. Only the words typed across the top of the screen.

"A mirror image," Jenny concluded. "Meaning if it confronts you, you will be fighting yourself. Well, not really. But, yeah."

"Dude, like in Witchcraft and Warriors," Brandon jumped in.

"Exactly," Jenny confirmed.

...*You have 15 seconds to withdraw your challenge*...typed the words across the screen.

"Everybody ready?" Tyler asked.

"Hell, yeah," Brandon replied, as everyone reached for their headsets.

...*your time to withdraw has expired*...

...*weapons equipped*...

...you may select weapon upgrades upon a confirmed kill of your opponent...

"Alright, everybody spread out!" Mike exclaimed. "Put your headsets on."

In unison, they all put their headsets on in anticipation of experiencing a combat game in virtual reality. They had played countless times as a team and arguably the best of the best as gamers. But this was a little different. Virtual reality was a new technology, an unknown and as of yet mostly unavailable technology. It would be challenging for certain, but a challenge they were all up to and eager to embrace.

"I don't see anything," Brandon shouted.

"Just wait a second," Tyler returned.

Suddenly, the virtual world appeared in front of them.

Elizabeth's eyes sprung to life. The gateway her grandmother had foreseen was open. Within seconds, the black shadow of her soul was sailing through the realm of eternal darkness toward a single pinprick of light. In the vast expanse of the abyss it was barely noticeable, almost resembling a dimly lit lone star in space. Every moment that had passed in her confinement she had relived the life she once had in her thoughts. Over and over countless times she had recounted every life event, until the desire for being alive again became insatiable, maddening her to the near point of insanity. Now as she approached the gateway, she could taste the living on her salivating lips. As she neared closer, she could feel the energy tugging at her very being, drawing her in. And then suddenly, with a violent burst of light, hell was behind her. She was on the other side.

White replaced the absence of light, a shade that had become foreign to her in a world of darkness. The intensity was blinding. She could feel her grandmother's presence, and the sound of her voice welcoming her back as her clouded vision slowly subsided.

"These are the fools you spoke of I presume?" Elizabeth growled with anger, displeased seeing strangers violating the sanctity of her home, watching Tyler and his friends oblivious to her presence.

"Precisely," her grandmother's shifting apparition noted.

What they were doing was beyond her comprehension, but it was unmistakably the source of the gateway she had come through. It would have to stay open. Countless souls occupied this realm, content to deny their fate and exist only in spiritual form. She was not one of them, nor would she ever consider to be. She had a plan. True, it was Hallow's Eve and the chance of others following her through was considerable, but that didn't concern her. The Gatekeeper, however, that was another matter altogether. Sooner or later they would learn of her escape and come to take back their prize. But the witching hour would be over shortly, and the veil between the living and dead would be too thick for them to pass. It was a chance she was willing to take.

"Kill them and close the gateway," her grandmother insisted.

"The gateway stays open," Elizabeth rebutted, much to the fury of her grandmother.

"Once again, you are being reckless child!" her grandmother chastised her.

"Indeed," Elizabeth's image smiled wickedly. "And I shall enjoy playing this...game."

They were standing in a white brightly lit room about the size of the parlor. In fact everything was white, from the floor to the walls to the ceiling, making it hard to determine where one end of the room started and the other ended. It had the faint sound of an echo when you spoke.

"Not much for graphics," Steve noted, looking around and seeing Phil, Brandon, Mike and Tyler spread out as best they could within the confines of the space allowed. They were all holding medieval swords of standard length at their sides, as they each began taking practice swings.

"It's weird," Mike stated, while swinging it casually in the air. "You can actually feel the weight."

"Jenny can you hear us?" Tyler asked.

"Yes," Jenny replied. "I'm standing at the front of the room, by the windows. You guys look so funny swinging what I assume is a sword that I can't see."

"Stay sharp guys," Brandon jumped in. "Any second now."

No sooner had he said that, a loud piercing scream came from seemingly nowhere as a ghost-like figure emerged from the white wall in front of them. It was lightning fast and came flying out at them immediately. They could see for just a second her skeleton face, with glowing blue eyes, screaming that horrible blood curdling sound and almost smiling at them. Her black clothes were tattered and whipping along with her long gray hair in the air. She was holding a shiny butcher knife in her hand, but didn't appear to have legs beneath her skirt. It was Ghostess. And then with a blink of an eye she disappeared.

"Where did she go?" Mike yelled, as all of them held their swords in a defensive manner and began turning around in different directions.

"Right here," came a woman's voice from behind Phil.

"Wait, what? It can talk to you?" Brandon asked in disbelief.

"Shit!" Phil exclaimed, spinning around immediately and raising his sword to strike. Only it wasn't the ghost he had expected to see. Instead it was a beautiful blonde woman.

"You don't want to do that," she spoke in a soft and lustrous voice. "It's just a game."

Phil stood motionless, still holding the sword above his head in strike position. But he could feel the weight of it straining against his muscles as his arm began to shake.

"There are other things we can do here also you know," she whispered, as she leaned towards his ear and put her hand over his hand that was holding the sword, and slowly lowered it down.

"She's tricking you bro," Brandon yelled from across the room.

"Aww, I'm not trying to trick you sweetie," she returned, now face to face with Phil and staring into his eyes. "I just want a little kiss."

There was something about her eyes. He couldn't explain it, but they were irresistible. It was as if they were drawing him into her. Their lips grew closer and closer, until you could hear the clang of his metal sword hit the ground as it fell, and they embraced.

"He's kissing someone?" Jenny asked in disbelief. She couldn't see anything going on in the game, but she could see the motions they made. And he was clearly kissing someone. "What the hell?"

"I think Phil has a new girlfriend," Brandon joked to Jenny.

Phil couldn't believe how real it felt. Her lips were so soft, like no other girl he had ever kissed. He could feel himself becoming aroused as the kiss grew more passionate and then...

"Ahh!" he screamed in horror, immediately reaching for his stomach and dropping to his knees.

In an instant, Ghostess had pulled the butcher knife she had hidden in her hand behind her and slashed Phil's guts wide open, spilling his organs onto the white floor in a pile of blood.

"Oh my God!" Jenny screamed, seeing Phil drop to the floor quivering in his own blood.

"Oh, shit," Brandon yelled out, running over to Phil. "Is this real?" he screamed. "Is this real?"

"It's real!" Jenny screamed back.

Brandon ripped his headset off, followed by Mike, Tyler and Steve and saw Phil lying on the floor. There was blood everywhere. And then in an instant, a huge gash appeared across the top of Brandon's shoulder, spewing blood into the air.

"Fuck, I'm cut!" Brandon screamed, reaching for his shoulder and seeing blood running down his arm.

"What is happening?" Jenny screamed, dropping to her knees and shaking, reaching for Phil's headset.

Brandon struggled to put his headset back on as Mike, Steve and Tyler had just done, and saw Ghostess fly almost like a blur past them.

"I'm going to kill that bitch," Steve shouted angrily.

"What the fuck kinda game is this Tyler?" Mike exclaimed.

"Not one you're very good at," Ghostess replied, appearing in front of them, only this time in skeleton form.

"We'll see about that," Brandon returned, as he saw Jenny, sword raised and coming up quickly from behind.

"Ahh!" Jenny screamed with anger, swinging the sword with all her might across the neck of Ghostess, decapitating her with ease.

Mike, Tyler, Steve, and Brandon watched as her skeleton head rolled across the floor, turning into the beautiful blonde woman's face she once was as it came to a rest. Jenny stood there trembling, partly in shock and still holding the sword in swing position.

"Fuck this game," Steve said, taking his headset off and walking over to the game console to end it.

…*confirmed kill*…typed the words across the headsets Mike, Tyler, Brandon and Jenny still had on.

…*weapons upgrade awarded*…

Suddenly the sword Jenny was holding disappeared and was replaced instantly with an AK47 automatic assault rifle.

Steve reached towards the game console and the eject button. Once he had his hands on it, he would smash it to pieces. But just as he made contact with it, a flash of lightning shot out from it so powerful it burnt his hand, leaving him screaming in agony.

"Goddammit!" Steve shouted.

"Now what?" Mike asked, raising the headset onto his forehead to observe.

"It won't let me turn it off" Steve explained, holding his hand. "I tried to eject it and…and I don't know…some sort of electricity shocked me.

Look at my hand dude. Shit, it hurts!"

Mike noticed his hand and grimaced. It had been burnt nearly to the bone.

"We got trouble guys!" Jenny shouted.

"Fuck," Mike said to himself, reaching to lower his headset.

"Just stay right here," he stated. "You can't fight. And stay away from the game," he added, with his headset now on.

...prepare for combat...

"Alright, look," Mike began to explain to the group. "It won't let us end the game. So we have to beat it."

"Are you kidding me man?" Brandon exclaimed. "Phil is dead dude. This is some serious shit."

"Looks like we only have to fight one at a time," Tyler acknowledged. "I don't know. Maybe we can beat it."

"Locked and loaded," Jenny said, holding the AK47.

And then suddenly the noise of a heavy chain dragging across the floor filled the room.

"It's Chain," Brandon said, with a lump in his throat.

"Jenny, take out his knees," Mike ordered calmly.

"Time to die," Chain said with a deep grumbling voice, appearing just as Ghostess did from the white wall in front of them.

"Now Jenny!" Mike yelled.

Jenny aimed the gun and pulled the trigger, sending bullets at a high velocity rate through the air towards Chain. But lacking experience shooting such a weapon, the gun kicked in an upward motion and rather than hitting its target, the bullets struck harmlessly into the ceiling above.

"Shit," Tyler and Mike said simultaneously.

"Who is it?" Steve asked, sitting on the floor and holding his hand.

"It's Chain," Brandon yelled back.

"I can do this," Steve thought to himself, reaching for his headset and remembering once again the game Dragonworld.

"What are you doing?" Tyler asked, seeing Steve in the game and struggling to hold his sword.

"Hey, shit face! Over here," Steve yelled toward Chain and rose to his feet.

Chain turned immediately in his direction and shot the long heavy black chain with a whip like motion directly towards him. Steve grimaced to hold his sword up but somehow managed. The idea was to catch the chain at the exact moment. The perpetual motion of physics should wrap the chain around the sword allowing him to yank back hard and strip the chain from the grips of its possessor. It worked countless times before in other games.

Unfortunately, even with both hands holding the sword up, he was losing his grip. Rather than the chain striking the fat part of the sword where it needed to, it glanced off the tapered edge, striking him firmly across the left shoulder and shattering his bones like toothpicks. In an instant, Steve dropped to the ground as his sword spun off into the air.

"Steve!" Jenny yelled out in dismay.

But before anyone could react, the chain whipped again. This time it struck him directly across his defenseless head, exploding it like a pumpkin across the white walls behind.

"Noooo!" Jenny screamed out. "You son of a bitch!" she screamed again, turning back to Chain and pulling the trigger of her weapon. Unlike the last time, her aim and command of the gun was true. Bullets penetrated and ripped the flesh and bones off both of his knees, collapsing him to the floor.

"Move in!" Mike yelled, as he, Brandon and Tyler raced to finish him off. But before they could get there, Jenny fired her weapon again into the black hooded cloak, expending her ammunition of countless rounds until the meter on her headset read zero, leaving what seemed to be a thousand holes into a now shredded and blood-soaked cloth.

...confirmed kill...

...weapons upgrade awarded...

"Now I have a grenade launcher," Jenny said, looking down at her gun.

"You're bleeding really badly," Mike acknowledged, looking at the gash on Brandon's shoulder and his blood-soaked shirt.

"Two down, three to go," he replied. "I'll make it."

"I never should have doubted you Jenny," Tyler said, turning to her.

"It's fine," she replied, wiping the sweat from her forehead. "But I can't believe Steve is gone." She wanted to cry. She wanted to just run away in her own misery. But she knew she couldn't. If she made it out of here, there would be time to cry. Not now.

...prepare for combat...

"Jesus, this game won't give up," Jenny said, with an exhausted voice.

"Not until you're all dead bitch," came a voice materializing into a human form directly in front of her and delivering a hard blow across her mouth, splitting her lip. It almost knocked her to the floor, but she stood her ground, spitting blood from the wound she had just incurred.

"Look familiar?" the woman said, reaching for her gun and stripping it from her hands unexpectedly.

It was Mirror, and she was an exact image of Jenny, down to every detail including her voice. Without hesitation Mike swung his sword, ripping her white blouse and inflicting a gash wound directly above her breasts.

"Shit!" Jenny exclaimed, reaching for her chest in pain and seeing the exact wound on herself.

"Hahahaha!" laughed the woman. "I'm her mirror you fool. What you see is what you get."

"Fuck me," Brandon said in disbelief.

"No, fuck her," Tyler returned, punching her so hard across the face it knocked both her and Jenny down at the same time.

"I'm so sorry Jenny," Tyler said, grabbing the gun off the stunned mirror image laying on the floor, and noticing a welt beginning to swell on the side of her face and Jenny's as well.

Within seconds though, the mirror image rolled over to Jenny, wrapping her arms around her and tumbling until it was impossible to determine who was who.

"Shoot her!" Jenny yelled, pushing her hand against what Tyler assumed was Mirrors chin, raising her head with a struggle for Tyler to get a clean shot. Tyler raised the weapon, making sure it was not in grenade launch position and prepared to fire.

"Are you crazy, Tyler?!" the woman with her head raised exclaimed. "I'm Jenny. Shoot her! Don't listen to her. She's trying to trick you. I'm Jenny."

"What do I do man?!" Tyler yelled out, his gun shaking. If this were like other virtual reality games with mirror images, only a direct kill would eliminate her without harming Jenny. His aim would need to be perfect, otherwise he risked severely injuring her.

"Uhhh!" the woman exhorted, as she head butted the other to escape from the grasp of her hand under her chin. Again they rolled in desperation, one fighting the other for control until finally one of them had the other in a headlock, fingers locked tightly around the others neck.

"Quit fucking around and shoot her!" yelled the one in control.

"I don't know! I don't know!" Tyler shouted.

Mike had an idea. Immediately, he began to desperately undo his bracelet hooked to his wrist as Tyler continued to aim the gun on both of them.

"Do you recognize this?" Mike asked, holding it in the air seconds after it came free.

"Yes!" Jenny cried out. "I gave that to you!"

"I gave that to you!" the other repeated.

And with that, Tyler pulled the trigger and put a single bullet right between the eyes of Mirror.

"She answered first bitch," Tyler said to her body lying motionless on the floor. Just then Brandon reached for Mike's arm.

"Dude, I'm not feeling so well," Brandon confessed, losing his grip on Mike's arm and crumbling to the floor.

"He's dying," Jenny said, scooting over to him on her knees and reaching to hold his hand.

"He's lost too much blood," Mike replied.

"Jenny," Brandon said, taking his hand in hers, his arm and white tank top saturated in red.

"I'm here Brandon," Jenny answered, squeezing his hand with Mike looking on and standing guard over them.

"You don't look so good," Brandon told Jenny, trying to keep his eyes open.

...confirmed kill...

...unauthorized use of weapon...

...no weapons upgrade awarded...

"I know," Jenny agreed, wiping the blood from her busted lip and starting to cry, ignoring the words she just saw printing across her headset.

"Jenny," Brandon spoke.

"Yes, Brandon?" Jenny answered, still holding his hand.

"Promise me you will beat this game," he returned. "Someone has to live."

"I don't know if we can," Jenny answered honestly.

"Promise me!" Brandon demanded, now choking on his words.

"Alright. I promise," Jenny agreed.

...prepare for combat...

"Can we pause it?" Mike asked.

"What?" Tyler returned.

"Can we pause it? Can we pause the game?" Mike repeated anxiously.

"I…I don't know," Tyler answered uncertainly.

"It's a game, right?" Mike asked again. "I mean, it still has to play by the rules."

"We'd have to do it manually…on the game console," Tyler stated, looking over at the remains of Steve, where at one point he had tried to stop the game.

"Let's try," Mike said, taking off his headset and walking over to it.

"Hurry!" Jenny yelled, as she stayed kneeling at Brandon's side and Tyler standing guard for the next opponent.

Mike approached the game box and saw the pause button. He reached out with his finger and instantly the box began to surge with blue sparks and electricity.

"I'm not trying to stop it, only pause it," he said out loud. But still the box remained enveloped in a blue haze.

"Godammit!" he yelled. "You have to play by the rules! I'm only going to pause it."

And with that the blue haze disappeared.

…*game paused…*flashed across Jenny and Tyler's headset simultaneously with Mike's finger on the button.

"It worked!" Tyler exclaimed.

…game will resume in 5 minutes…

"We've got 5 minutes," Jenny shouted.

"I see that," Mike replied, putting his headset back on.

"Woah, who the fuck is that?" he exclaimed, seeing Elizabeth appear out of nowhere in front of them. She was wearing a black dress with long sleeves accentuated with black lace that crisscrossed one another in a shoestring manner from her shoulders down to her wrists. Her hair was a fiery orange color that flowed in a straight line to just below her waist and was topped with a medieval style crown. You could see an astrological tattoo of some sort on her neck, but it was hard to make out as her hair was covering most of it. Both of her hands were marked with tattoos as well, strange in their design and concept. She was clearly a witch, of that they were certain, but beautiful nonetheless. More than likely she was in her early twenties. Most distinctive of all though were her eyes. They were of such a bright blue that they actually shined, almost as if they were made of glass.

"You are not welcome here in my house," she spoke with anger. "But since you are here, I am making this childish game you are playing more interesting."

"Who are you?" Jenny asked.

"You will all die," Elizabeth said, ignoring Jenny's question and looking down at Brandon to accentuate her point.

"Just let us stop the game, and we will leave," Mike pleaded.

"No," Elizabeth simply replied.

"He's dead," Jenny spoke softly, letting Brandon's hand go and resting it on his chest as she looked up at her with swollen eyes.

"Pity," Elizabeth acknowledged, without an ounce of remorse. "For how long have you treated my home as your personal playground?"

"I...we didn't know that..." Jenny struggled to get the words out.

"I have been absent for quite some time, this is true," Elizabeth looked down at her contemptuously.

Jenny could feel the evil spilling out of her. Every word she spoke and the way she spoke them made her skin crawl.

"But not anymore," Elizabeth hissed, as her eyes began to radiate with electricity, peering into Jenny's. "Finish your pathetic game! When your corpses are rotting on my floor, I have a use for it."

And with that she disappeared, leaving them staring at each other with expressionless stoned faces.

"This is your fault!" Mike shouted, turning around and pointing his sword at Tyler. You could see the anger building up in his eyes. Tyler said nothing. He just stood there with Jenny's gun to his side as Mike held the tip of his sword two feet from his chest. He knew it was his fault, but what could he say that would make anything better. Sometimes words fall on deaf ears.

"Do it!" he finally exclaimed to Mike. Mike remained motionless, his sword still in a thrust kill shot position

"Do it!" Tyler repeated.

"Stop it!" Jenny yelled, standing up. "This is bullshit. He's your friend!"

"We're all going to die anyway," Mike stated, lowering his sword and coming to his senses. "You heard her."

"It's coming, Mike," Jenny said, grabbing his arm. "There's only two left. Pull yourself together. We need you."

Mike stood silent for a moment, feeling defeated. But Jenny was right, there were only two left. The witch was obviously manipulating the game, but she couldn't change the fact that it was just that…a game. And games can be beaten.

"Why did it say…*no weapons upgrade awarded…?*" Mike asked Jenny.

"I think because it was my gun," Jenny replied. "Brandon used my gun to kill Mirror. The game knows that."

"What difference does it make?" Mike asked.

"You have to earn it," Tyler answered. "The gun is in Jenny's arsenal on her headset. Well, I mean Phil's headset."

"And I have a grenade launcher," Jenny added. "Next thing that shows up, I'm going to blow it back to hell."

"You can't do that," Tyler interjected. "We're too close."

"He's right," Mike agreed "You'd kill us all. So who's left?…Madeline and Zeltar, right?"

"Yeah," Brandon agreed, and Jenny shook her head to agree as well.

"If I'm right, then Madeline is next," Mike said, thinking out loud. "The game would save it's best for last. And zombies are easy to kill with a gun. One head shot and that's it."

"I can do that," Jenny said, "But I need my gun back."

Tyler handed her the gun he had used to kill Mirror with and bent down to pick up a sword laying on the floor.

"No, wait. That's not going to work," Mike said. "Whatever you do, don't kill her Jenny."

"I don't follow you," Jenny said confused.

"Me neither," Tyler agreed. "I mean the guns the easiest way. You even said it…one head shot."

"Yes, but if either Tyler or me kills her, we will get a weapons upgrade," Mike explained. "We'll have two guns to fight Zeltar with rather than one."

"He's got a point," Tyler stated.

"Stay out of this one Jenny," Mike said to her, touching her swollen cheek.

"Ouch," Jenny flinched.

"I'm really sorry about that," Tyler said.

…*combat will resume in 60 seconds*…

"Whatever you do…DON'T shoot," Mike reminded Jenny, as he and Tyler raised their swords.

"You take the left side, and I'll take the right," Mike told Tyler, as they assumed positions. "Jenny, you're the only one with a gun. So, she's probably going to come after you first. You're her biggest threat."

"So what do I do?" Jenny asked confused.

"Stay towards the back and let her get close. We will try and flank her," Mike ordered.

…*prepare for combat*…

"You were right. It's Madeline," Tyler said, seeing her appear through the wall.

She was definitely your typical female zombie, moaning as usual and walking with a limp. Drool was running down her open decayed mouth. At first she looked confused, pausing to look first at Mike, then at Tyler, and then directly at Jenny.

"Just stay back," Mike instructed. "Don't engage her."

Tyler took two steps back away from her to clear some distance.

"Aim your gun at her Jenny, but DON"T shoot," Mike said.

Jenny lowered and aimed her weapon. If she had to, if it came down to it, she would open fire.

"She's moving towards her," Tyler stated.

"Give her some distance," Mike replied. "She's not worried about us right now."

Mike and Tyler stood where they were, watching the zombie move closer and closer to Jenny.

"Mike?" Jenny asked nervously. The zombie was no less than ten feet from her, and she could see the hunger in its eyes.

"Just hang on," Mike tried to reassure her. They had to wait until the zombie was ready to strike. It was the only way to catch it off guard. Jenny had her hand on the trigger. She would fire anyway in seconds.

"Now Tyler!" Mike yelled.

Mike and Tyler ran towards the zombie and Jenny, swords raised and ready to swing. Just then the zombie made its move and lurched with a growling voice at Jenny's throat, teeth first like a mad dog would do. The timing could not have been more precise. Within a millisecond of Jenny pulling the trigger, Tyler had cut the zombie in half at the waist and Mike had decapitated its head.

"Holy shit that was close!" Jenny exclaimed, trembling and pushing the half torso off of her.

...confirmed kill...

...weapons upgrade awarded...

"Yes!" Mike shouted with joy, looking at the AK47 he was now holding.

"It worked! It worked!" he exclaimed, smiling.

"Zeltar's next," Tyler stated.

"I know," Mike acknowledged, realizing his victory was short lived.

"Pause the game," Mike ordered, bending over with one hand on his knee and his gun in the other. "I need time to think."

"Do you think she will let us?" Tyler asked. "The witch I mean."

"She will let us, just pause the game," Mike returned quickly.

"Alright, alright," Tyler replied.

Tyler removed his headset and did as Mike did moments before. Only this time the box did not resist the request, and he was able to hit the pause button with no consequences.

…game paused…

…game will resume in 5 minutes…

"So, any ideas?" Tyler asked, returning to Mike and Jenny and putting his headset back on.

"We have what…2 thousand rounds between the two of us?" Mike asked for confirmation from Jenny.

'Yeah," Jenny agreed.

"So, we hit him with everything we've got," Mike suggested.

"I'm not saying that won't work," Tyler began. "But just like any other game…well, one's that don't actually REALLY kill you…you have to have better weapons to kill the top dude."

"Like a grenade launcher," Jenny put in.

"Yes," Tyler agreed.

"What about weakness points?" Mike asked. "A lot of games you can kill him with a sword strike down the back of his neck."

"He's almost 7 feet tall," Tyler stated. "How am I supposed to get that kind of position for a strike?"

"Get him on the ground maybe?" Mike suggested. "Shoot the hell out of him and drop him to his knees."

"I don't know, that might work," Tyler reluctantly agreed.

"I think we're going to get bloody on this one though," Mike stated.

"It's the last opponent," Jenny said. "We can win."

"What if we shut off the power?" Tyler asked.

"It won't let you. You saw what happened to Steve," Mike replied.

"I don't mean the game. I mean the generator," Tyler answered back.

"Everything in this room is in the field of play," Mike answered. "If you even tried to open a door, even with your headset off…it will fry you."

"Well, it's gotta run out of gas sooner or later," Tyler said in desperation.

"Not soon enough," Mike said back.

…prepare for combat…

"Shit," Tyler said.

"Time to die," came a voice that sounded like a man that had taken way too many steroids.

"Yeah, I've heard that before," Mike acknowledged, as the beast, like the others, appeared from the white wall in front of them. He was even bigger than the image the game depicted of him. He looked like a monster you would see in a movie where a top secret experiment had gone terribly wrong, leaving him half man and half something else. Not even half man actually. He looked as if hell itself had just opened the door and let him in.

"He's terrifying," Jenny cried out.

"Just pretend it's just a game. He's not real," Mike said.

"This isn't JUST a game!" Jenny shot back. "And he IS real!"

Without hesitation or a second to take in what was happening, Zeltar launched his massive battle ax with a sideways motion, slicing through the air with every rotation.

"Get down!" Mike yelled, as all three of them dove to the ground head first, their weapons slamming with them against the floor with a metallic sound. The battle ax nearly grazed them but instead landed harmlessly into the white wall behind them.

"Fire!" Mike yelled, seeing the giant now approaching them with a fierce ferocity, determined to rip them to shreds.

Mike and Jenny jumped to their knees and opened fire.

"Stay down!" Mike yelled to Tyler.

With both weapons firing at the same time, empty shell casings began accumulating in a heap on the floor like hail falling from the sky. Zeltar stopped in his tracks and was knocked back a step from the sheer magnitude of bullets penetrating his gray skin.

"Keep shooting!" Mike yelled. "Give him all we got."

Tyler laid still on the floor with both hands covering his ears and his sword next to him. The sound of the AK47's firing relentlessly was almost deafening. As the bullets continued to pound the monster, they were beginning to have an obvious effect. Zeltar collapsed to one knee, holding himself up with his arm. His skin was torn and shredded across most of his massive body and partially across the face, leaving what appeared to be one eye missing. Blood oozed from every hole and had begun to drip through the crevices of its jagged teeth and down its mouth. Considering the amount of damage he had sustained, it was surprising he was even standing at all. And then just like that, with a snap of a finger, there was silence.

"I'm out," Mike stated, looking at his ammo count.

"Me too," Jenny replied.

"What now?" Tyler asked desperately. "He's still alive!"

Zeltar was indeed still alive. Not only was he still alive, but his wounds were slowly closing up one after the other.

"I don't believe it," Mike said with dismay, looking on as Zeltar healed himself.

"Shit," was all Jenny could add.

"Mike, it's now or never," Tyler said standing up. "The grenade launcher," he added looking at Jenny.

"Give me your gun," Mike ordered Jenny.

"What?" Jenny asked, confused. "But you said…"

"There's no time!" Mike interrupted, dropping his gun with a crash to the floor and grabbing hers from her arms. "Get behind me and Tyler," he barked, switching the gun into grenade capability.

Jenny hesitantly agreed and stood directly behind them as Mike lowered the gun towards Zeltar.

Its wounds had almost completely healed now, and it had begun to rise from its crouched position.

"Now Mike!" Tyler yelled.

"I always loved you," Mike said, turning around quickly to look at Jenny one last time and then pulling the trigger. The grenade launcher fired with a roar and within seconds Zeltar exploded into a ball of flames, sending bits and pieces of him in every direction and splattering onto the walls like paint balls. Almost simultaneously, the shock wave of the explosion burst through the air, lifting Mike, Tyler and Jenny ten feet off the floor. It was as if a cannonball had hit them squarely in the chest, slamming them hard against the wall behind them and then dropping them like dead weights to the floor. All three of them lay motionless while words began to type across their headsets.

...*confirmed kill*...

...*game over*...

The screen went blank momentarily and then began typing again.

..*score results*...

...*opponents killed*...5

...*players killed*...5

...*TIE*...it typed one last time before going blank permanently.

5

THE AFTERMATH

"Against the warnings you ventured in haste,
Ashes to ashes, now your souls lay to waste."

Nighttime continued to pass in the now silent room, until giving way to a small beam of light fighting its way through the small cracks of boarded up windows and onto a blood soaked wooden floor, occupied with bodies lying in the position in which they fell. Near the front of the room was Mike, Tyler and Jenny. Tyler laid on his back, arms stretched outwards and his eyes wide open. Mike had come to rest on top of Jenny, his arms and legs broken and in a backwards twisted position.

All you could see of Jenny was one arm stretched out from underneath Mike and a converse shoe. The generator had quit running long ago, spitting and spewing for more gas before finally shutting off. To the back of the room, near the door and the decapitated body of Steve, stood the stand, game console and screen, already covered in newly made webs.

Earlier that morning...

"Do you know where Mikes at?" Mike's dad asked Chris, walking into a farm building where Chris was shoveling hay.

"I thought he was here," Chris stated, stopping what he was doing to lean on his shovel and wipe sweat from his forehead.

"He ain't," Mike's dad answered. "I've been trying to call him. I told that boy his ass better be home early."

"You mean he didn't come home last night?" Chris asked, knowing he had bought beer for Tyler and Mike last night.

"How the hell should I know?" Mike's dad replied angrily. "But he ain't here now, is he?"

"It's not like Mike not to come home," Chris stated, becoming concerned.

"I knew I shouldn't have let him go," Mike's dad returned. "Kept rambling on about some damn Halloween party. Probably passed out drunk somewhere."

"I know a few places where he and Tyler hang out," Chris said. "I mean, if you want, I can go look for him."

"Yeah, alright," Mike's dad agreed. "But listen," he added, pointing a finger. "If you find him, tell him he better get his ass here to work."

"I'll tell him," Chris agreed.

That was hours ago. Since then, Chris had been driving around every place he could think of trying to find him. But there was one place left to look. He had remembered Tyler telling him about an old abandoned house on Crabtree Road that he, Mike and some friends partied at.

"Damn, why didn't I think about that before?" Chris asked himself, slapping the steering wheel of his old beat up Chevy farm truck. Crabtree Road was across town. He used to deliver hay to a farm down that road, but that was years ago before a fire burnt it to the ground. Now there was nothing on that road but the old house. He knew exactly where it was. Chris turned the truck around, making a U-turn in the middle of the street and headed in that direction. Twenty minutes later came a sound breaking the eerie silence the room of the old house possessed. It was the sound of tires rolling slowly over gravel, and the faint sound of an engine. This went on for several seconds before stopping and then followed by the sound of a truck door slamming.

"Mike, Tyler?" Chris called out, seeing Mikes 69 Chevelle and two other cars parked unattended alongside the gravel driveway.

"Your dad's gonna kick your ass bro!" Chris yelled out towards the old house to Mike.

"Mike's dad was right, damn kids are probably passed out," he said to himself, as he began walking and reaching for his phone. "I found him," Chris said after reaching Mike's dad.

"No, I haven't seen him yet, but his car is here. I'll keep you posted," he returned into the phone and then placed it in his back pocket.

Chris made his way up to the house and followed the path of beaten down weeds leading to the generator and back door.

"Smart kids," he said out loud, seeing the generator and extension cord leading to the house.

"Mike, Tyler?" he shouted out again, reaching for the knob to open up the door.

What he saw when he opened it was unimaginable, unthinkable even.

"Oh my God!" he cried out. "Oh my God!" he repeated even louder, with a hand over his mouth as he surveyed the carnage and blood soaked floors.

"Shit!" he exclaimed, his hands reaching immediately for his phone and trembling. He could barely retrieve it from his back pocket yet alone dial 911, but somehow he managed.

"911, what is your emergency?" the voice from the phone asked.

"I'm on Crabtree Road…uh…outside of…outside of Beckon County," Chis tried to get out. "Something terrible happened…I…I don't know… they're all dead!"

"Who's dead, sir?" asked the voice.

"All of them!" Chris shouted. "There's blood everywhere. Oh my God!"

"Okay, just try to stay calm," the voice stated. "Officers are on the way. Do you know the address, sir?"

"They've been…they've been butchered!" he continued, shaking uncontrollably. "One of them doesn't have a head."

"Just calm down," the voice repeated. "Officers are on the way and will be there soon. Do you know the address?"

"No…uh…it's…it's an old abandoned house. It's the only house on this road," he answered.

"Alright," replied the voice. "Are you in the house at this time?"

"Yes," Chris answered.

"Okay, I want you to leave the house immediately," ordered the voice. "Wait for the police outside."

"Okay," Chris complied.

"Help," came a voice from across the room, or at least that's what Chris thought he heard. It was very faint and sounded like a female.

"Help," he heard again, only just slightly louder.

"Someone's alive!" Chris shouted into the phone to the dispatcher. "I can hear her."

"Okay, help is on the way sir," replied the dispatcher. "But I need you to leave the house."

"Where are you?" Chris asked, ignoring the request and looking around the room.

"Oh God!" he exclaimed, seeing what looked like Mike laying on top of someone towards the front of the room.

"Over here," the hoarse and barely audible female voice replied. It was coming from that direction, underneath Mike.

Chris ran over to her as fast as he could, not knowing what to expect but that at least, for now, she was alive.

"I'm sorry Mike," he said, as he carefully pulled his deformed and broken body off of the girl trapped beneath him.

"Jenny!" he exclaimed the moment he saw her face. She was beaten and bruised with a huge welt and split across her cheek and had a busted lip. Her arm appeared to be dislocated from her shoulder and three of her fingers had been broken and bent in an awkward position.

"Sir, are you there?" came the voice from his phone.

"Thank God you're alive," he said

6

THE INSTITUTION

"Beware of thy leap into the unknown to start anew,
Your willingness to follow
foreshadows that which is waiting for you."

Five years later…

Dana stood in front of her mirror, turning sideways to get a better look and not convinced she liked how her new dress fit.

"I don't know. Do you think it makes me look fat?" she asked her friend Rachael, as she adjusted the lace straps on her shoulders.

"You asked me that like three times already at the store," Rachael sighed, concentrating on painting her toenails and not even looking up.

"Well they always look better when you're trying them on there," Dana returned. "Maybe they use fake mirrors or something."

"Fake mirrors?" Rachael asked with a jest.

"Yeah, you know…like fun house mirrors," Dana added, fiddling with her hair. "Only they make you look thin and you buy the dress. Then when you get home and try it on, you look fat as shit."

"Okay first of all, you don't look fat," Rachael said, finally looking up.

"And second, I think you're reading way too many conspiracy theory books."

"Speaking of…" Dana said, giving up on the mirror and reaching for a magazine laying on the desk beside her. "Did you see this?" she asked as she tossed it on the bed next to where Rachael was sitting.

"No, what is it?" Rachael asked, too preoccupied with her toes to even look.

"Game World Magazine," Dana answered, sitting down on the bed and picking it up.

"Aha," Rachael acknowledged with no interest.

"Listen," Dana pleaded.

"I am listening," Rachael replied.

"So…" Dana continued, opening up the magazine to a specific article. "Remember Mike Zimmerman?"

"Not really," Rachael answered, while she painstakingly painted her last toe nail.

"Oh c'mon!" Dana exclaimed. "Mike Zimmerman! He was ranked number one in the world."

"Wait, I remember," Rachael answered, finally looking up. "Wasn't he the guy that got killed by a drunk driver five years ago?"

"That's what they want you to think," Dana answered. "But that's not what really happened."

"So you're saying it was a cover up?" Rachael asked sarcastically.

"Exactly," Dana returned.

"I should have guessed," Rachael said dryly. "Dana…"

"No seriously listen," Dana pleaded.

"Dana…" Rachael repeated.

"Please just listen," Dana pleaded again.

"Okay, I give up. I'm listening," Rachael replied exasperated.

"So…'" Dana continued, ignoring Rachael's tone and turning a page to begin reading the article. "Five years ago there was a tragedy and our gaming community lost Mike Zimmerman, a world record holder and second place finisher at the 2014 National Championship, to a drunk driver. But is that what really happened or was there something darker, more sinister involved? We sat down with Jenny Aldren, a gamer and Mike's partner during that championship, for an exclusive interview. What you will hear is shocking."

"Interesting," Rachael agreed. "Let me see that," she said, reaching for the magazine.

Rachael was a gamer herself. Well maybe not quite as serious of a gamer as Dana was, but they had played together since the 8th grade and were the best of friends. She vaguely remembered Mike Zimmerman, but then she didn't pay as much attention to world ranks and things like that as Dana did.

"So you expect me to believe that a game did this?" Rachael asked, after reading the article and emphasizing the word *game*. "A game not only killed Mike but four other gamers, brutally I might add, in some old abandoned house in the middle of nowhere?"

"Yes!" Dana exclaimed.

"Dana, the woman who claims this…what's her name?" Rachael began.

"Jenny," Dana obliged.

"Jenny," Rachael continued, "is in a mental institution. I mean c'mon, what's that tell you?"

"Did you read where that old house was?" Dana asked.

"I don't know," Rachael admitted, glancing at the article again to read.

"Crabtree Road," Dana stated with the answer.

"So," Rachael stated flatly.

"So, I know where that is," Dana said. "It's like ten miles from here, just outside of Beckon County."

"Wow, really?" Rachael said, surprised. "Wait a minute," Rachael added after a second, having an idea where this was going.

"Do you know how much that game could be worth if we found it?" Dana asked. "THE game that killed Mike Zimmerman and four other gamers. It's legendary now in the game world. Everyone on the internet's talking about it."

"It doesn't exist Dana," Rachael said emphatically.

"The police covered it up, because they never found the killer," Dana continued. "And the murders were so gruesome, they didn't know how to explain it. But Jenny did, down to every last detail. I mean, how can you make that stuff up?"

"She's in a mental institution...hello?" Rachael said, waving her hand in the air to remind her.

"Only because she tried to tell the police what happened and they didn't believe her. They thought the shock from what had happened... I mean what she had been through, made her insane," Dana tried to explain. "Didn't you read the article?"

"And it probably did," Rachael agreed. "But that doesn't mean monsters from some virtual reality game killed everybody."

"I want to talk to her," Dana said.

"Who, Jenny?" Rachael asked.

"Yes," Dana answered.

"You don't even know where she's at for one thing," Rachael stated. "And even if you did, what are you going to do? Just walk in and say... hi, my name is Dana. I'm nobody, but can I talk to a mental patient of yours."

"I'll say I'm a reporter," Dana shot back.

"Aha...an 18 year old reporter with final exams next week," Rachael said sarcastically.

"Shit, I gotta go," Dana realized, seeing the time on the clock and reaching for her purse. "Justin is probably outside waiting already. Hey thanks for babysitting my little brother for me," she added, opening up her bedroom door and walking out.

"No problem," Rachael replied with a worried look on her face and reached for the magazine again.

"Hey sweetie," Dana said to Justin as she opened up his car door to climb in. Dana was a tall girl at 5'11, but her long legs tended to make her look even taller, especially when she wore high heels as she was now. She had the cutest dimples when she smiled, and the most amazing eyes. Eyes which were sometimes green and sometimes blue, depending on how the light hit them. Today at this moment, they were blue. She had experimented with different hair colors. She was a brunette last summer, but decided her natural blonde hair suited her best.

"Hey sweetie pie," Justin smiled back, watching her climb in. "I like your new dress."

"You don't think it makes me look fat, do you?" she asked.

"Of course not," Justin answered, reaching over to give her a kiss. "So, I guess you were able to talk Rachael into babysitting," he said, as he leaned back in his seat to start the car.

"Piece of cake," Dana replied.

"You look good too," she added, noticing his crisp black suit and tie.

"Well thank you," Justin said graciously. "But I gotta tell you, I feel a little weird in this suit. I'm just not used to wearing dress clothes."

"I know, but it's only for tonight," Dana smiled, as Justin pulled the car away. "And my parents will be happy you came for their anniversary party."

"Yeah your parents are pretty cool," Justin said.

It was only about a twenty minute drive through Beckon County to downtown. Normally Dana would have taken advantage of the leisure time, rescuing her bare feet from the cumbersome high heels she was not used to wearing and propping them up on the dashboard while she rummaged through the internet, catching up on the daily social gossip waiting to be discovered on her cell phone. Rummage the internet she did do, but it wasn't gossip she was interested in. Instead she found herself searching for the location of the Beckon County Municipal Institution.

"What are you doing Dana?" she thought to herself, clicking on a link that matched her search. She had done some crazy things in her life, some she was proud of and some not so much, but this was beyond rational. When she blurted out for Justin to take exit A without even thinking, she realized just how irrational she was. Of course, he was confused and argumentative. After all, the exit to their destination to meet her parents was in the opposite direction of what she was proposing. He would understand eventually. There was no time to explain it now. The only thing that mattered to her at the moment was getting to the mental institution. Not long after, following more directions from Dana, Justin pulled the car into what was marked as visitor's parking and turned off the engine.

"Why a mental institution?" he asked, confused, with his finger still on the key. "Are you crazy?"

"That's not funny," she shot him an irritated look. "I need to talk to someone. I'll explain later. Oh and probably better you wait out here," Dana quickly spoke as she noticed Justin starting to exit the car.

"Dana, I'll roast out here in this suit," Justin complained. "And I can't sit with the air condition running…it will overheat."

"Alright," Dana agreed. "Come with me then."

Dana and Justin walked up a set of stairs to the main entrance doors and stepped inside. The air conditioned building offered relief from the summer sun that had made Justin sweat even from such a short walk. Justin pulled and tugged at his clothes, as if they were smothering him, while Dana scanned the hallway for a registration desk.

"Down there," she said, finding it and pointing in its direction. Whether they would let her see Jenny was another question altogether. She pondered that thought over the sound of her high heels echoing against the empty hallway and the scuffle of Justin's shoes following behind her. Maybe Jenny wasn't even here in the first place.

"May I help you?" a woman of dark color and about in her sixties asked, placing a finger on the rim of her thick framed glasses and slightly lowering them down her nose.

"Just don't say anything," Dana whispered, turning back to Justin. "I told you I will explain later."

Justin shoved his hands in his pockets like an innocent bystander and stood by patiently listening to the receptionist barking out orders for an ID and a thousand questions with a tone to him that seemed like she was either overworked, underpaid or both. Dana fumbled through her purse to hand over the ID while she slid the nylon stocking lined toes of her foot from her high heels and rubbed the back of her adjoining ankle. It was a subtle nuance of hers he had grown accustomed to seeing her do when she was nervous.

"I'm a friend of hers," she lied with her best gleeful smile, watching as the woman's fingers were busy punching the keyboard on her computer.

"Aldren?" the woman asked, not impressed, spelling it out to verify and briefly looking up at her before typing it in. .

"Yes, that's correct," Dana replied.

This was a plan destined to fail, she thought to herself as the sweat began to accumulate on her eyebrows. What person claims to be a friend but yet hasn't visited once in the five years since she's been incarcerated. It was such a bad idea that only got worse when the woman informed her that they did in fact have a Jenny Aldren, but that she had requested no visitors.

"Please ma'am, I really need to see her," Dana begged.

Begging wasn't exactly protocol in a mental institution, but it did work. After hesitating for a moment and a leering eye, the woman agreed to take her to see Jenny.

"Follow me," she said, coming out from behind her large desk. "But he will have to wait here."

"I'm sorry," Dana said looking at Justin. "I won't be long."

"It's fine," Justin agreed. "I'll just…ah…I'll just wait right here doing nothing I guess," he said exasperated, not knowing what to do with himself. The woman informed him that there was a small waiting room off of the lobby where they came in and that he was welcome to wait there. Grateful to be able to sit down, Justin headed back to the lobby.

The woman led Dana down a long hallway to an elevator, her high heels joining chorus with Dana's making a clicking sound that echoed against the empty walls. Dana could feel the anxiety building up in her throat as the elevator opened to the 3rd floor and they exited.

"Right down here," the woman pointed to another hallway as Dana followed behind her before coming to a door marked room 413.

"Miss Aldren," the woman called out, as she took a key to unlock the door and announce herself. "Miss Aldren, I have a visitor here to see you," the woman declared. She walked in while Dana stood in the hallway, her arms folded across her chest and breathing heavily.

"I specifically requested no visitors," Dana could hear a voice from inside the room say with irritation.

"She says she's a friend of yours and that it's important," the woman stated.

"A friend?" Jenny asked with a laugh. "My friends are all dead."

"I understand," the woman replied, as she turned away and began to walk back to the door.

"Wait," Jenny said quickly. "Let her in."

"You may see her," she said to Dana with a suspicious look on her face, exiting the room and sidestepping to allow Dana to slide through.

Dana walked anxiously into the room. Jenny was sitting in a chair next to a table with only an ashtray, a pack of cigarettes, and a lighter occupying it. An unlit cigarette hung from her mouth.

53

Taking a look around without being too obvious, Dana quickly realized interior design was not exactly a priority. The walls were soft white, with the only color in the room coming from blue and purple curtains framing a single window that offered a boring view of the parking lot below. An open paperback book rested on the bed, which appeared to be challenging for anyone with a height advantage to sleep in. Behind it stood a reading lamp, adjusted to a precise angle and hovering over the headboard. With the exception of a calendar pinned to the wall and flipped to the incorrect month of October, there was nothing even remotely interesting.

"I don't know you," Jenny said matter of factly, reaching for the lighter and observing the unfamiliar face of Dana as she stood by the door. She was younger than she had expected her to be, barely out of high school at best. Why she was here made her eyebrow arc in an inquisitive fashion.

"Well, come in," Jenny said, with a motioning gesture to Dana and lighting her cigarette.

"I didn't know they let you smoke in here," Dana stated, trying to start the conversation and fidgeting with her clothes. That was already the wrong thing to say.

Obviously this girl was nervous, but surely she didn't come to a mental institution to discuss smoking policies. "And you came here just to tell me that?" Jenny asked, blowing out a puff of smoke in defiance.

"No, sorry," Dana answered. "I'm just…well I'm a little nervous."

"Nice dress," Jenny acknowledged looking Dana over. "What's the occasion?"

"Oh, thanks," Dana replied, looking down at her dress to smooth out the wrinkles. "Well, it's my parent's 20th anniversary party. I'm actually supposed to be there right now."

"But instead you decided to just stop by a mental institution and say hi to me," Jenny stated with sarcasm.

"Well, no…I mean not exactly," Dana said. It was such an awkward moment for her that she was already thinking that perhaps coming here wasn't one of her best ideas. She could feel the tips of her fingernails digging into her skin as she clenched her fists with anxiety, struggling for something to say.

"Do you have a name?" Jenny asked.

"I'm so sorry," Dana answered, still very nervous and reaching out her hand. "Dana."

"Nice to meet you Dana," Jenny acknowledged, leaning out of her chair to shake her hand. "I'm Jenny, but then you obviously already know that. Cigarette?" Jenny asked, reaching for the half empty pack on the table.

"I don't smoke, but thanks," Dana returned.

"Well, I didn't either," Jenny stated, taking a drag and exhaling before continuing. "So, what can I do for you Dana?"

"I read your article in Game World magazine," Dana stated as a starting point.

"You're a gamer," Jenny smiled.

"Yes!" Dana answered. "Well…compared to you I'm sure I suck, but yeah definitely a gamer. I got my picture taken with you and Mike, and you both signed my magazine."

"Really?" Jenny interjected. "You were at the world championship?"

"Yes!" Dana answered. "Well I was only 13 then, but I remember it like it was yesterday. Anyway, I'm sure you don't remember me."

"Sorry, no." Jenny admitted, flicking her cigarette into the ashtray. "There were so many people there. You're right though, it does seem like it was just yesterday." She could even picture her and Mike sitting together at the signing booth, Tyler looking on as fans lined up in droves, each one sharing their own version of admiration for them. He would occasionally flash a fake smile her way but that did little to mask the contempt he had for her. She remembered how that had made her feel…like a traitor. After the competition, when they had placed second…his stare could have burned holes through her. She should never have agreed to it.

"Mike Zimmerman is practically a legend now." Dana stated. "Did you know to this day nobody has ever held a number one world ranking for as long as he did?"

"Actually, no. I didn't know that," Jenny admitted, taking another drag of her cigarette and pausing for a moment to reflect.

"I broke up with him shortly after that," Jenny continued.

"Now that I didn't know," Dana admitted. "What happened?" she asked, before realizing it was an inappropriate question. "I'm sorry, I shouldn't have asked that."

"No, it's fine," Jenny assured, waving it off. "I wasn't good enough. I knew that, and he knew that. Of course, he would have never told me that or admitted that I shouldn't have been his partner at the world championship. But I mean, we all knew it, especially Tyler."

"Oh, c'mon," Dana jumped in. "You're awesome!"

"Not at that level," Jenny replied. "Not when you're competing against the best in the world. Anyway, I was holding him back," she said, butting out an expired cigarette and pulling a new one out of the box.

"So, that's why you broke up with him?" Dana asked, not really understanding. "Because you were holding him back?"

"Dana, when you game professionally there's money involved," Jenny tried to explain. "Sometimes potentially a lot of money. He would never have had the heart to tell me he needed a new partner. So, I broke up with him."

"Did you still love him?" Dana asked, becoming wrapped up in the story.

"Of course I did," Jenny answered, still holding the unlit cigarette and grabbing the lighter. "I still do," she added, after it came to life and added fresh smoke to an already smoke filled room. "You're not a reporter or something are you?"

"No!" Dana reassured her.

"Yeah, you're too young to be a reporter anyway," Jenny said, satisfied with Dana's answer.

"Actually, I was going to say I was if they wouldn't let me in to see you," Dana confessed laughing. Jenny laughed as well.

"So you were pretty determined to see me," she stated, feeling more comfortable with Dana now.

"Usually once I get an idea in my head, yeah I'm pretty determined," Dana agreed.

"I have to admit, it's been awhile since I had such an avid fan," Jenny said.

"Actually..." Dana began, "that's not the only reason I'm here."

That immediately wiped the smile off Jenny's face, but then she should have known better. Happiness didn't belong in a place where they try to convince you it's not a prison, regardless of how much you think otherwise.

"So go on then, tell me," she said, leaning back in her chair and folding her arms across her chest. "What's the real reason why you're here?"

"Is the game still there?" Dana asked bluntly.

Jenny took a long drag on her cigarette, pondering Dana's question for what seemed like a several minutes before answering it. "I don't know, probably," Jenny finally answered. "My guess is yes."

"Where did it come from?" Dana asked.

"Why do you want to know so much about this?" Jenny asked with suspicion.

"Because I want to help," Dana returned.

"Help with what?" Jenny asked, still not really understanding.

"Help prove that you're not crazy, that you shouldn't be in here," Dana answered sincerely.

"Dana," Jenny started, "I really appreciate that. Really, I do. But there's nothing you can do. Nobody will ever believe what really happened."

"I'm here, aren't I?" Dana asked. "I believe you."

Jenny sighed. She almost felt pity for Dana. Not even the reporter that interviewed her shared that kind of conviction. Probably none at all, actually. Jenny agreed to the interview for a chance…finally…to tell her side of the story. But in the end, the truth didn't really matter. It was about selling a magazine. That was it. "Shit," was all Jenny could respond with. "I honestly don't know what to say."

"Where did it come from," Dana asked again.

"Tyler told us some guy gave it to him at the convention, the same one you were at," Jenny conceded and gave in to Dana's questions. "But that's all I know."

"Did you see it?" Dana asked. "Because someone had to have manufactured it. Even if it was a prototype like you said in the article, the software company that developed it has to be on the game cartridge somewhere."

"True," Jenny admitted. "But I didn't see it. Well I saw it, but not close up and it was dark anyway."

"I want to go to the house and look for it," Dana stated.

"No!" Jenny exclaimed, standing up from her chair. "It's too dangerous. That house is creepy. I never liked it."

"I'll be fine," Dana said.

There was something about that house. Something that didn't sit right with Jenny. She always felt it, every time they went there to party and game. Something in that house was not what it should have been. She remembered the witch and what she had said, "You are not welcome here in my house." She also remembered her warning that they would all die.

"No it won't!" Jenny exclaimed.

"Jenny, right now that game is the only proof you have," Dana assured her.

"That game needs to be destroyed," Jenny shot back.

"And it will be," Dana agreed. "You can destroy it yourself after we research it if you want. But it's not safe there. What if someone else finds it and decides to play it?"

"I've thought about that," Jenny agreed. "I've even thought that if I ever got out of here, I would go and get it myself. But I don't think I could ever go in that house again. And besides, there's more to it than just the game."

"What do you mean?" Dana asked.

"I don't know," Jenny replied. "Maybe it was just the game. I'm not really sure."

"Then I will get it for you," Dana said. "If it's still there, I will get it and bring it to you."

"You're going to go whether I agree or not, aren't you?" Jenny asked.

"Yes," Dana said. "But I wanted your approval."

"Why?" Jenny asked.

"Because I respect you," Dana answered without hesitation.

"I still don't get it," Jenny said. "Why? Why do you want to do this? I mean, I get that you're a fan and all of that, but you don't even know me. Why would you come here when you should be at your parent's anniversary party, ask me all of these questions and want to get involved? I really don't get it."

"Ever since I was a kid, probably...I don't know...ten years old," she said, brushing the hair from her eyes. "I always wanted to prove people wrong," Dana began to explain. "My dad says I should be a lawyer, but that's not me. I'm really, pretty much a conspiracy theorist. I'm a gamer, yes, but more so the other. That's probably why I'm such a good gamer. You know....trying to solve or unlock the next level. There's always something right in front of you that most people can't see."

"This isn't a game, Dana," Jenny interjected. "And it's not a conspiracy theory. It's evil. You have no idea what you're getting into."

"Well, I agree that it's evil," Dana admitted. "But it's definitely a conspiracy, or else you wouldn't be here."

"Your dad's right. You should be a lawyer," Jenny conceded.

"Exactly," Dana admitted. "But yeah, that's definitely not me. Honestly, it's true…I am a fan, and that does have something to do with it… but without me, I really don't see anybody helping you. I really don't."

"Alright, alright," Jenny repeated herself with a show of hands in defense, realizing there was no way to talk Dana out of what she wanted to do and knowing in her heart she truly didn't want to. "The game box is in the back room of the house on the main level. All of the other doors are boarded up, so use the back entrance. But by now it's probably boarded up too."

"Okay," Dana acknowledged.

"And there won't be any power," Jenny continued. "So you're going to have to take the box too. You won't be able to eject it."

"So, I won't even know if the game is inside until I get home and turn it on," Dana confirmed.

"Yes," Jenny agreed. "Dana, whatever you do, do not push the play button."

"Gotcha," Dana replied. "I will go tomorrow in the afternoon. I think it should be safe."

"Put my number in your phone," Jenny said. "If something happens… if something goes wrong…I want you to call me, okay?"

"Yes, of course," Dana agreed, grabbing her phone out of her pocket to type in the number. "Don't worry, nothing's going to happen. It's been five years."

"Yeah, that's what worries me," Jenny mumbled under her breath.

"What?" Dana asked, not hearing what she had said.

"Nothing," Jenny said, dismissing it. "You should go, don't keep your parents waiting."

"Yeah, true," Dana agreed. "Alright, see you tomorrow then?"

"See you tomorrow," Jenny answered.

"Wait," Dana said, turning to walk away and then stopping. "I feel like I should give you a hug or something."

"That's sweet," Jenny said. "Why not?"

The two of them embraced in a short hug, while Jenny whispered the words "be careful" in Dana's ear.

7

THE HOUSE ENCOUNTER

"Heed my words or pay the price you shall,
Thy last breath will be taken,
To this I avow."

The following afternoon....

"Crabtree Road should be coming up," Dana instructed Justin from her memory.

"How do you even know about this place?" Justin asked, while keeping an eye out for a street sign.

"My granny used to take me to a farm there when I was a kid," Dana answered. "We would go almost every weekend during the summer to pick strawberries."

"That's nice," Justin said.

"Yeah, it's a great memory," Dana reflected, thinking back to that time and imagining herself carrying an empty wicker basket into a field full of unpicked strawberries. "But then about a year or two later there was a fire and the whole place burnt to the ground," she added.

"Damn, that sucks," Justin admitted.

"Yeah," Dana agreed, still visualizing everything in her head. "I remember driving past the old abandoned house. Every time we went by it, I would stare at it and imagine how it must have looked when it was new and how beautiful it had to have been."

Justin slowed down as he spotted a worn out sign that was barely legible reading Crabtree Road and made the turn, creeping the car along with the sound of gravel crunching beneath his tires. He questioned how far down the house was, as he steered clear of potholes that seemed to dominate what one would argue as being considered an actual road. Nodding to Dana's reply that it was at least a couple more miles, he thought about everything she had informed him of. It wasn't that he didn't believe her story, quite the contrary. This just didn't seem like such a good idea.

"It's just an old house," Dana stated, noticing the anxiety on his face.

"People died in that house Dana," he glanced over at her.

"Do you know how many people live in houses that someone died in?" she asked. "And most of the time they never even know it."

"Yeah, until they become haunted," Justin rebutted.

"Sometimes," Dana admitted. "But they are not all always evil."

"Your parents are probably in Hawaii by now," Justin said, trying to change the subject.

"Lucky them," Dana said, agreeing. "Maybe on our 20th anniversary we will be there," she added, smiling over at him.

"What, when were 38?" he said sarcastically. "I don't even want to think about being that old."

"That's not old!" Dana said, surprised he would think that.

"We haven't even graduated yet," Justin stated. "So to me…yeah…that's a long way off."

Dana sat there and pondered that for a moment. Wondering where in life she would be at that age.

"Damn, there's literally nothing on this road," Justin said, steering the car around potholes now and then. "Maybe the house isn't there anymore. Maybe they tore it down."

"It's there," Dana said, seeing it now in the distance.

"I see it," Justin agreed.

They were too far away to make out much of its appearance, but you could easily see three massive chimneys, one on each end of the house and one in the middle, towering from the roof into the sky. Being the only house along the road, it stood out in a sense that it demanded attention.

"It really doesn't look much different than I remembered it," Dana observed as they got closer.

"It's huge," Justin said. "Do you know how old it is?"

"My granny said it was built in 1862 during the civil war. So that makes it what…about 150 years old?" Dana said, doing the math in her head.

"And I thought 38 years was old," Justin conceded.

Dana continued to stare in awe as the house grew bigger through the windshield. She had always been most fond of the massive two story columns stretching from one end of the house to the other, still standing in all of their majesty, disobedient to time. Even the plantation shutters refused to let go of their hold, some still in place but missing several slats, some hanging desperately from their steel anchor, completely intact. Pine trees filled the landscape, surrounding the house like caretakers watching over it, their needles littering its moss covered roof and their branches caressing it.

Justin wondered if he could even get in the driveway, noticing the waist high weeds that had completely overtaken it.

"Just park here," Dana suggested. "We can walk."

Justin parked his car facing towards the entrance of what used to be a gravel driveway, and along with Dana he exited the car.

So, wearing shorts was definitely a bad idea, Dana admitted to herself, feeling the course dried up weeds brushing against her pale white legs as they started to walk through them.

"How do we get in?" Justin asked, seeing the boarded up front door and windows.

"Jenny said around the back of the house," Dana answered, swatting bugs from her face as they flew from the disturbed weeds.

"Great, so we have to walk all the way through this stuff," Justin complained, swatting the bugs as well. "Wow, look at the side of the house. It's almost completely covered in vines."

"My legs are going to be covered with scratches and bug bites," Dana said looking up.

"I told you to wear jeans," Justin said.

"It's too hot for jeans," Dana shot back.

"I hope there aren't snakes or something in here," Justin thought out loud.

"Now why would you have to say that?!" Dana exclaimed, fighting her way through what had now become even thicker weeds. "I already can't wait to take a shower."

"I don't know. Just saying," Justin answered.

"Almost there," Dana said with gratitude, approaching the back of the house.

Justin noticed what appeared to be some kind of machinery buried in the thick weeks and brushed them aside to get a look. "It's a generator," he noted.

"They used it for power when they gamed here," Dana explained. "So, the door must be right around the corner."

Dana and Justin turned the corner and stood in front of the back door Jenny had mentioned. But as expected, it was completely boarded up. And there were no windows nearby except for the second story.

"Now what?" Justin asked, scratching his leg from bites.

"Try to pry on this one," Dana said, touching one of the boards that seemed to be at least somewhat rotten. Dana and Justin put both of their hands on the board that had been nailed horizontally across the door and pulled with all their might, breaking it free from the left side.

"Twist it back and forth," Justin suggested as they did just that, finally breaking it free completely and leaving four corroded and rusty nails protruding out. "Four more to go. All we have to do is use this board for leverage, put it behind the others and pull." With a little effort, one by one, his idea worked and within minutes they were inside.

"It's darker in here than I thought it would be," Dana admitted. "We should have brought a flashlight."

"Yeah, you're right," Justin agreed. "It smells so musty in here," he said, breathing in the stagnate air and looking around. "So this is it? This is where they played the game?"

"Yeah," Dana said looking around in awe as well. "Maybe if we pull one of these curtains down we could see better," she suggested, walking slowly towards the front of the room. Dana approached a boarded up window draped with heavy curtains from its time and gave a hard yank, bringing it instantly crashing to the floor with a loud thud as it kicked up a cloud of dust, filling the room within seconds. Justin began gagging and reached for his shirt to cover his mouth.

"Well, at least we can see," Dana said, gagging and coughing as well.

"There it is!" Justin exclaimed through his shirt, pointing toward the back of the room. With the tapestry gone from the window, all that remained were four five-inch wide boards nailed horizontally across it in the same manner as the back door had been. But there was plenty of space between them to let the afternoon sunshine in, easily highlighting a cobweb covered stand, game console and monitor screen towards the back of the room.

"Daaaaaanaaaa," softly whispered a voice that seemed to come from nowhere.

"Did you hear that!?" Dana exclaimed, standing still and listening.

'Hear what?" Justin answered. "I didn't hear anything."

"I could have sworn I heard something," Dana stated, not moving.

"Daaaaanaaa," it whispered again.

"That! Did you hear that?" Dana exclaimed.

"No, but you're freaking me out," Justin admitted.

"Is someone here?" Dana yelled out, her voice echoing through the empty house as she waited for a response.

"Can we just grab the box and go?" Justin asked anxiously.

"Play the game Dana," a voice said, only this time slightly louder than a whisper.

"I heard it!" Justin exclaimed, turning to face Dana directly. "It sounded like it said play the game."

"Let's get out of here," Dana said, running over to the game box with Justin right behind her.

"We have to disconnect everything," Justin said, dropping to his knees on the floor and grabbing it.

"Play the game Dana," a female voice said clearly.

"Hurry!" Dana exclaimed.

"I am hurrying!" Justin yelled, his hands now shaking and fumbling with the wire connections to detach them.

"*PLAY THE GAME BITCH*," appeared on the screen monitor in front of them written in the dust that covered it.

"Fuck this," Dana said, grabbing the game box from Justin's hand, two wires still attached and ripping them loose, knocking the screen monitor over in the process. "Run!" she yelled.

Justin and Dana ran to the open door as fast as they could. Justin was in the lead as the door began to slam shut. Meeting it with full force and almost knocking him backwards into Dana, they managed to make their way back outside, not stopping as they once again battled the thick overgrown weeds.

"I told you this was a bad idea," Justin yelled back from in front of her.

"Just keep going!" she yelled, struggling to keep the game box in her hands and feeling something cut into her legs.

It didn't take her long to realize what it was. The weeds had suddenly sprung to life, twisting and turning like snakes. They began wrapping themselves around both her and Justin's ankles and legs. Within seconds, they had metamorphosed into a thick and entangled thorn briar patch.

"Shit, we're in a thorn patch!" Justin exclaimed. "I'm stuck."

"Me too!" Dana shouted.

"I don't believe this!" Justin yelled out angrily, seeing his car parked a mere ten feet away.

It was no ordinary thorn patch. It was so dense that the branches resembled cooked spaghetti, one entwined around the other and covered with thorns the size of shark's teeth.

"We have to try and break free," Dana cried.

"What and get ripped to shreds?" Justin asked, knowing what the consequences would be.

"It's going to hurt like hell, but unless you have any other suggestions," Dana stated.

"Alright, I'll go first," Justin said reluctantly. "Here goes…" Justin pushed against the entwined branches with his body, feeling what seemed like hundreds of small razors ripping the flesh from his legs instantly. Whatever or whoever was in that house did not want them to leave. Cringing from the pain, he tried to work himself free. Dana looked on helplessly with tears beginning to form in her eyes. Soon it would be her turn. Making some progress but realizing not enough, Justin had an idea.

"What are you doing?" Dana asked, seeing Justin pulling his t-shirt over his head.

"I need to use my hands to try and pull some of these branches away," Justin explained, wrapping the shirt around one hand to form a makeshift glove and beginning the task. The idea did work, and before too long he had made it to the car, but not without paying a price. In the process of pulling the thorn infested branches aside, many of them had drug across his bare chest, inflicting him with dozens of deep gashes. Sweat mixed with blood covered his body, and he could feel it running down his legs though his tattered jeans.

"Alright, now it's your turn Dana," he said. As much as she wanted to, that she knew she had to, she froze. Seeing the end result of Justin's chest, as he stood there bleeding, petrified her. She could see that he had cleared a lot of it away, but she would still get cut, that was for certain. Maybe not as bad, but that thought offered little reassurance to her shaking legs that hesitated to move.

"I can't. I can't do it!" she cried.

"You have to do it Dana!" Justin demanded. "Throw me the box first."

"I'll try," Dana said, grabbing it with both hands and tossing it to him like a soccer ball. It wasn't a pretty throw, as it tumbled recklessly through the air, but it somehow managed to end up in Justin's waiting hands.

"Now, just push with your legs and try to ignore the pain," Justin coached her.

"Okay," Dana agreed, wiping the tears from her eyes. Dana pushed with her legs again, while trying to lift them from the branch's grasp.

"Oh God!" she groaned while the razor-sharp thorns did their damage. Tears streamed down her face, mixed with a combination of her own perspiration and running eyeshadow, painting her with a helpless look of desperation. If it weren't for Justin's insistence to keep pushing, she would have refused to move another inch. "It's cutting the shit out of me," Dana cried.

"You're almost free," Justin tried to assure her.

Seconds later Dana had in fact worked herself free, but she still had to manage her way through the patch Justin had partially cleared. Justin instructed her to lift her knees up as she walked through it, which did help somewhat.

"Look at my legs!" Dana exclaimed, looking down at the gashes the thorns had made and the blood running down to her socks.

"You'll be okay, just get out of there," Justin begged.

Dana continued trudging through, lifting her knees up as Justin suggested, until finally reaching him.

"I made it!" she cried, wrapping her arms around him.

"I knew you could do it," he said, kissing her head as it rested on his shoulder. "Let's get out of here."

Justin threw the box onto the back seat. No sooner had both of them shut their doors, he had the car started and its tires spinning, kicking up dust and gravel as it took off. Dana hesitated but couldn't help herself, and took one last look at the house as they drove away. Unmistakably she could see a pair of glowing blue eyes staring out at them through the second story window.

"You're bleeding badly," Justin said, looking down at Dana's legs while his car tore down the desolate road towards the highway.

"So are you," she replied, looking at his bleeding chest.

"I've got some bottled water and I think some rags in the trunk," Justin said. "But I think we're going to have to go to the hospital."

"I'm sorry Justin," Dana said reaching for his hand. "I mean, for involving you like this."

"Are you kidding?" he asked. "There was no way I would have let you go there alone."

"Thanks," she said with a smile. "Jenny was right about the house."

"Yeah, I think that's a given," Justin agreed.

8

PLAY AGAIN

"Mirror, Mirror on the wall,
Your fate is least understood by you of all."

Several hours later...

"Well, at least no stitches," Dana said, walking with a limp into her parents' house. Justin followed her and placed the game box on the counter.

"Yeah, I just feel like a mummy with all these ace bandages wrapped around me," Justin said. "And you look like one," he added, teasing her about her own partially wrapped legs.

"It's actually harder to walk with the bandages than it is with the pain," Dana said, as she plugged in the game box and hit eject.

"Bingo," she said, pulling out a black game cartridge as it ejected and unplugging it almost at the same time. "We got it," she said, turning around and holding it up for Justin to see. "I gotta call Jenny. I wonder where Rachael and David are?" she thought out loud, dialing Jenny's number on her cell phone.

"Ice cream," Justin answered, holding up a note Dana had missed from Rachael laying on the counter next to the game box.

71

"Jenny!" Dana exclaimed, while nodding her head to Justin that she sees the note reading 'went for ice cream. Be back later, Rachael'.

"Dana! Oh my God, I was starting to worry," Jenny said right away. "Did everything go okay, did you get it?"

"We got it!" Dana said with excitement. "But we did run into some problems you might say."

"What happened?" Jenny asked with concern and stood up from her chair immediately.

"I'll explain later," Dana promised. "I'll be there in about 30 minutes."

"There's a really bad storm coming so be careful," Jenny informed her.

"Okay, see you soon," Dana said, clicking off her phone.

"I gotta get my laptop," she said to Justin, putting the phone in her back pocket. "Why don't you just stay here and rest. I can take my car."

"No, I'll drive," Justin replied.

"Are you sure?" Dana asked. "I mean really, it's no big deal. I'll be fine."

"No! After what happened so far today, I'm not letting you out of my sight," Justin said emphatically.

"You're sweet," she smiled, kissing him quickly before heading for her room to grab her laptop. "I can't find it anywhere," Dana said, returning several minutes later.

"The news says a really bad storm is coming," Justin said, opening the refrigerator and watching the TV he had just turned on.

"Yeah I know, that's what Jenny said," Dana acknowledged, looking aimlessly through the kitchen for her missing laptop.

"So maybe we oughta just call it a day and go tomorrow," Justin suggested, reaching for a pizza box he had just discovered.

"No, I'm not leaving that game in this house," Dana said adamantly, but noticing the pizza box Justin was pulling out.

"Oh my God, Rachael bought that pizza!" she exclaimed. "She'll kill us if we eat it."

"We'll buy her another one," Justin said, placing it on the counter and opening up the box to reveal an almost full pepperoni and sausage pie.

"I still need my laptop," Dana said, grabbing a slice and taking a bite as if she hadn't eaten in days.

"You're not even going to warm it up?" Justin asked, noticing her hunger.

"Mmhmm…no," she answered, with a mouth full of food. "Uh, I'm so starved," she continued talking while chewing.

"Yeah, me too," Justin agreed, reaching for a slice and foregoing the warm up process as well.

"So maybe Rachael used your laptop," Justin offered, while chewing and talking at the same time as well. "Check the game room. She always hangs out there."

"Good idea," Dana said, swallowing. "She is always getting into my shit."

"And maybe you should change clothes?" Justin suggested.

Dana put her forefinger up, as a gesture to signal a pause, while she took the last bite of a quickly devoured slice and then spoke. "No time for that," she said, reaching for another slice.

"Your socks are covered in blood," Justin pointed out.

"Well, you don't look so great yourself," Dana stated, biting into her second piece of pizza and addressing Justin's shredded jeans and blood stained shirt.

"True," Justin admitted, finishing his first slice of pizza not quite as quick as Dana had.

"I'll go look," Dana said with regard to her laptop and taking the pizza with her.

"I got it," Dana said, returning only a moment later from the game room with the laptop in her hand and a piece of crust in the other.

"Alright, come on," Justin said, wiping the pizza grease off on his shirt and hitting the remote to turn the TV off.

"Wait, I need something to drink," Dana said, tossing the crust in the trash can and opening the refrigerator once again to grab a bottled water. "Want one?"

"Yeah, sure," Justin said.

Dana handed him one before closing the door and then grabbed her laptop. "Let's go," she said satisfied.

Justin set the TV remote on the table and followed Dana to the front door, closing it behind them as they left. He was anxious to beat the storm coming and didn't even realize the game cartridge remained lying next to the box on the kitchen counter.

"We can go to the zoo next time Hun," Rachael said to David, turning the key to Dana's parents' house and opening up the front door.

"But I wanted to go today," David whined.

"I know, but it looks like a really bad storm is coming," she said, as they made their way inside and closed the door behind them, locking it as well.

"I'm thirsty," David said.

"Alright, what would you like?" Rachael asked, throwing her keys on the kitchen counter and almost hitting the game cartridge. "How about an apple juice?"

"Okay," David said.

"I see Dana and Justin were here," she said out loud to herself, seeing the pizza box left out on the table. "They could have at least put it away," she added, lifting up the box lid to observe what was left. "Rachael grabbed the box with one hand and with the other opened the refrigerator to put it away, retrieving a boxed apple juice for David in the process. Rachael didn't mind babysitting at all. In fact, as an only child from a divorced family and growing up around Dana and her family, being at Dana's parents' house almost felt like home. Really in a way too much like home. David was, in her eyes, as much her little brother as if he were blood. Her own mom was rarely ever there for her. She worked two jobs, except occasionally on the weekends. But then that never offered her much quality time together, because her mom would rather go to bars and drink the night away on her time off than even consider doing something with her. Dad was a completely different story. She hadn't seen him since she was 10, maybe younger. She really couldn't remember the last time she saw him, nor cared to. He was what she referred to as a career alcoholic. She did have a few good memories of him before the bottle replaced anything that should have been important in his life. But that was then and this was now. She accepted that. Dana and her family brought peace and some kind of stability into her otherwise wrecked world. However, she did sometimes envy Dana. Well, not because Dana was so tall and slender and good looking. She would never match her in that way. She had worn glasses since she was five and although she never had a weight problem, she was not blessed with the natural beauty Dana had. That was fine with her. She looked, in her opinion, 'average'. Average was good. It was just that Dana seemed to have the perfect life. The perfect boyfriend, the perfect parents, and all that comes with it. She was always left to clean up after her, even something as trivial as putting away a pizza box, and sometimes that irritated her.

"So what would you like to do tonight hun?" Rachael asked, handing David his apple juice box as he hopped onto a slightly higher stool than his size would allow.

"Cartoons!" he said, grabbing the remote laying on the table in front of him and clicking it on.

"That's not cartoons, that's the news," Rachael stated as it came on.

"I know. I'm not dumb or something," he said, ready to switch the station.

"Wait!" Rachael exclaimed, seeing a weather forecast warning flashing across the screen.

"High winds, torrential downpours and lightning expected. Stay indoors or take cover," it read.

"That's not good. Maybe I should call Dana," Rachael said, reaching for her cell phone.

"She's probably kissing and smooching with Justin," David said.

"Hmm, and how do you know about that stuff little guy?" Rachael asked, teasing and rubbing his head. "Well, my phones dead anyway."

"They do it all the time," David said, using his hand as a prop and mimicking the two of them kissing.

"Haha," Rachael laughed. "Well, one day you will have a girlfriend to kiss and smooch," she said, leaning over to plug her phone in next to the game box and paying it no attention.

"Yuck!" David exclaimed.

"Alright, I'm going to take a quick shower," Rachael said, as David became engrossed in a cartoon now playing.

"Watch your cartoons and don't get into anything, okay?" she asked. "David?" she asked again for his response.

"Uh huh," he finally answered, sipping on his juice with his eyes glued to the TV.

Rachael watched him for a second, and then walked upstairs to take her shower.

Fifteen to twenty minutes later, with the cartoon ending and a commercial beginning to play, David plopped down from what to him was a tall chair and headed towards the refrigerator. It was, after all, a commercial break and what better time than now to replenish his empty apple juice box with a new one. But his attention was distracted in the process. "Oh cool," he stated to himself, noticing the black game cartridge and box on the counter. "Dana got a new game!" David grabbed the game cartridge, holding it in his hand and flipping it over several times before he was satisfied it would play in the game box downstairs.

Dana and Justin...

"Shit!" Dana exclaimed out loud, making Justin jump in his car seat.

"What?!" Justin asked nervously from her outburst.

"I forgot the frickin game!" she said, not believing she had forgotten it.

"Are you serious?" Justin asked, also in disbelief. "We're like two minutes away. I thought you took it?"

"No, all I carried out was my laptop," Dana returned. "Oh my God, I can't believe I forgot it," she said, putting her hand on her forehead.

"Well, what should I do?" Justin asked, driving and already looking for an exit to turn around. "What if Rachael or David finds it?" he pointed out, turning his head to look at her. 'What if they play it?!"

"We have to go back, now!" Dana realized panicking.

Justin took the next exit that was available and thankfully only a mile away, redirecting his car in the opposite direction. "This doesn't look good," he said, seeing an ominous huge dark cloud developing through the windshield.

"I need to call her," Dana said with a worried voice and quickly grabbed her cell phone.

"C'mon, answer dammit!" she yelled into her phone as her call rang numerous times unanswered.

"Just call the house number," Justin said, turning his wipers on as the rain began to fall.

"I can't call the house!" Dana said with anxiety. "My parents don't have a landline anymore. Didn't you know that?!"

"Sorry, no," Justin answered. "How should I know that? You're the only person I call."

"Why isn't she answering her phone?" Dana asked with frustration. "Can't you drive faster?" she asked, becoming annoyed.

Justin pushed on the gas pedal to speed up, but the acceleration the car made was short lived as the rain now became a torrential downpour, making it hard to see the road in front of them and forcing him to slow down considerably. "I can't even see where I'm going," Justin said, leaning towards the windshield as if that would help.

"If they play that game…" Dana started.

"They won't…right?" Justin asked, hoping for some reassurance while trying to keep the car between the lines on the road he could barely see.

"She will," Dana confirmed. "If Rachael sees it she will. I know her."

To make matters worse, the storm was intensifying. Heavy winds were now pushing against the car, making Justin fight the steering wheel with both hands clenched on it with a death grip. Lightning was striking in all directions, as other cars on the highway began to pull over to the side, surrendering to Mother Nature.

"Dana, we have to pull over. This is crazy," he stated, noticing the other cars doing the same.

"If they play that game, they will die!" Dana yelled back. "We can't stop!"

Back at the house…

"Hold on a second little guy," Rachael said to David, returning from her shower just in time to see him leaving the kitchen with the game in his hand.

"Where did you get that?" she asked.

"In the kitchen," David answered simply. "Dana must have brought it home. She brought a game box too, but I don't need it. It'll fit in the one downstairs."

"Can I see it?" she asked.

"Sure," David answered, handing it over to her.

Rachael took the cartridge from him looking for a game title, but there wasn't any. All she could conclude, recognizing from its shape, was that it was a virtual reality game.

"Well, if it's Dana's then put it back where you found it please," she said, handing it back to him. "You know you're not allowed to play her games."

"But why not?" he asked reluctantly, going to return it.

"Because they're adult games. They're not for little boys," she explained. "If you want to play something, why don't you go up to your room? You have tons of games up there."

"Alright," he conceded. "Can I have another apple juice?"

"Yes, but don't spill it," Rachael agreed, heading to the refrigerator.

David headed to his room, while Rachael fixed herself a soft drink with ice.

"Funny I didn't see that before," she said to herself, taking a sip and staring over at the game box laying on the counter in clear site.

"I wonder if my phone is charged?" she thought, reaching for it.

"Twenty percent…that's it?!" she asked impatiently. "I gotta get better chargers," she said, setting it back down and deciding to let it charge more. Grabbing the game cartridge, she flipped it over a couple times once again to check for a title. Concluding the obvious, curiosity got the best of her. "Well, there's nothing else to do," she thought, heading to the game room downstairs with the cartridge in her hand.

Dana and Justin…

"Somethings not right," Dana said, ending another unsuccessful call to Rachael. "She should have answered by now."

"We're almost there," Justin said, still fighting the relentless storm. "Look for our street sign, it should be coming up. I can't see shit."

Just then Dana's phone rang.

"Rachael?!" she asked, answering it immediately and not even looking to see who the call was from.

"Huh? No, it's me, Jenny. Is everything okay? It's been over an hour now."

"Yeah, um… no we're fine," Dana tried to hide. "We uh…we had to pull over. The storm was so bad we couldn't even see to drive."

"Alright," Jenny said, not convinced by the tone of Dana's voice. "Be careful, okay?"

"We will, thanks," Dana answered. "Be there as soon as we can."

"Okay, bye bye," Jenny said, hanging up.

"Bye, Bye," Dana replied, doing the same.

"Right there!" Dana exclaimed, barely seeing the street sign identifying the road to her neighborhood. "We're four blocks away," she said with relief.

Back at the house...

Rachael powered up Dana's VR set and inserted the game, waiting for it to load while she grabbed a headset.

TIME TO DIE came across the screen in bleeding letters.

"I should have known," Rachael said to herself. "One of Dana's zombie games."

...select number of players... typed across the screen followed by keyboard numbers ranging from 1-10.

"One," Rachael said, pressing the screen.

...accepted...

"This must be an old game," she noted.

...choose your zone...

Rachael touched the screen to bring up boundary zone options. She was very familiar with this kind of format, but it was definitely outdated.

"20x16 she typed into the simulated keyboard, easily knowing the room measurements from countless games she and Dana had played there together.

...too small for mortal combat...

...do you wish to proceed?...

"Yes," Rachael typed in.

...your opponents...

Rachael watched as the game went through a list of gruesome and evil looking characters, followed by what read...

...HIGH SCORE...

...2014...

...opponents killed...5

...players killed...5

"2014? Five players killed? OH MY GOD!" Rachael yelled, remembering the article Dana had shown her in Game World magazine. "Dana got the game!" she exclaimed in horror. "This is the game!"

...prepare for combat...

"I don't want to play!" she yelled, as a sword appeared in her hand.

"No, please!" she pleaded, dropping the sword and reaching to take off her headset. "I don't want to play!!!"

"Too late," came a voice from a woman that was her identical twin, materializing right in front of her. It was Mirror. She looked just like Rachael, only her eyes and the smile on her face was from that of a demented person.

"Not smart to concede your weapon," Mirror said with that awful smile.

"I'm sorry. I don't want to play," Rachael said, standing there terrified with her headset still on. "Please don't hurt me."

"Pick it up," Mirror demanded.

"I don't want to," Rachael said, imagining the circumstances if she did.

"I said pick it up bitch!" Mirror demanded, smacking Rachael across her face with an opened hand and an incredible force.

Rachael dropped to her knees, shaking and in tears, knowing she was about to die.

"You're pathetic," Mirror said, reaching out with her hand and wrapping it around Rachael's throat. "Just like your friend Dana."

"Dana," Rachael tried to cry out. "Help me."

"Help you?" Mirror asked, as she lifted Rachael up from her knees by her throat and raised her off the floor.

"Your own God can't even help you," she said, with Rachael's feet dangling in the air and gasping for breath.

...Dana and Justin...

"Stop the car! Stop the car!" Dana said, yelling and opening her door before Justin could pull in the driveway.

"Rachael! David!" she began yelling immediately and running for the front steps.

Just then a bright flash lit up the sky, followed by a bolt of lightning that came streaking down, striking a pole and its transformer no more than 20 feet from Dana. The transformer exploded and sent power lines crashing onto the street below in a fireworks display of sparks and blue flames, convulsing like an injured snake on the water in which they had landed. In that exact moment all the electrical power in Dana's parents' house shut off, ending the game Rachael had unfortunately played and vaporizing Mirror into thin air, dropping Rachael to the floor.

"Holy shit!" Justin yelled out after the explosion and jumped out of the car as fast as he could.

"Dana! Where are you?" Justin yelled, calling out for her. "Are you okay?"

At that point, Dana had already reached the front door and was fumbling with her keys to try to unlock it when she heard his voice.

"I'm okay," she yelled out in his direction. "I'm at the front door," she informed him, turning the key to the door as the water ran down her face, blurring her vision and relentlessly pounding her on the back.

"I'm right behind you!" Justin yelled.

Dana had just opened the door as Justin arrived and slammed it shut, silencing the deafening sound of wind and rain.

"Rachael? David?!!" Dana began to yell, as she ran to where she had a sinking feeling she would find them...the game room.

"I'm up here!" David cried out from upstairs.

"Go get him," Dana instructed Justin. "I know where Rachael is."

"But I'm not…" Justin began.

"Please, just go get him," Dana asked, with the look of a drowned rat. "He's scared."

Justin quickly climbed the stairs to the second level and ran to David's room, while Dana dashed through the house to the basement stairs leading to the game room. But with the power off, the staircase and the basement were pitch dark.

"Rachael, are you down there? Are you okay?" Dana yelled down, realizing she was going to have to find a flashlight. There was no response from Rachael.

"Just hang on. I'm coming," Dana yelled again. Dana rushed to the kitchen, frantically pulling open a cabinet drawer and rummaging through its cluttered contents. She couldn't see very well, but she remembered her dad kept a flashlight in there for emergencies.

"Thank God," she said to herself, feeling the flashlight and grabbing it.

"On my way Rachael," Dana yelled, turning on the flashlight and heading for the stairs. All this running wasn't doing her injured legs much good. She could feel the pain through her bandages, but at this point she didn't care. Running down as fast as she could, Dana approached the last step and turned the corner, shining the flashlight into the game room and finding Rachael on the floor motionless.

"Rachael!!" Dana screamed, sliding to the floor beside her.

"Dana," Rachael whispered with a hoarse voice, slowly coming around from her unconscious state.

"I'm so sorry baby. I'm so sorry," Dana began to cry, setting the flashlight down and carefully removing the headset Rachael was still wearing.

"It was the game," Rachael tried to talk, feeling the effects of nearly being strangled to death and a swollen welt forming across the side of her face.

"I know. I tried to call you. I tried to warn you," Dana said in tears and caressing Rachael's hair.

"My phone was dead," Rachael explained. "It was choking me to death and then I passed out," she continued in a raspy voice. "What happened?"

"The power went out from the storm," Dana explained. "It stopped the game. Does it hurt to talk?" Dana asked, seeing the black and blue bruises around her neck.

"Yes," Rachael answered.

"Alright, I'm calling an ambulance," Dana said, reaching for her phone from her back pocket.

"Dana, no!" Rachael said, grabbing her arm. "There's no way to explain this."

"Dana?!" Justin yelled down from upstairs, hearing her voice in the otherwise silent house. "Is Rachael okay?"

"Can you come down here please?" she yelled up.

"Stay right here buddy," Justin said to David. "It's too dark down there, okay?"

"Alright," David agreed.

Justin carefully maneuvered down the darkened staircase to the game room.

"Oh my God!" he exclaimed, seeing Dana on her knees with Rachael.

"She's okay," Dana assured him as he approached. "It tried to strangle her," she stated, shining the flashlight on Rachael's neck and trying not to blind her. "I want her to go to the hospital, but she says no."

"Does it hurt to swallow?" Justin asked Rachael.

"Yes, a little," Rachael agreed.

"Then you need to go," Justin said quickly back.

"No!" she exclaimed the best her voice allowed her. "Can you two just help me up, please?"

Justin and Dana carefully helped her to stand, each holding her to make sure she had her balance.

"Are you okay?" Dana asked before letting go.

"Yeah, I think so," Rachael said, trying out her standing position. "Just a little woozy."

"I still think you should go to the hospital," Dana insisted.

"What and end up in a mental institution like your new friend Jenny?" Rachael said slightly bitter. "No, thank you. Damn, that bitch hit me hard," Rachael acknowledged, touching what she could tell was a swollen cheek.

"Who was it?" Dana asked. "Do you remember?"

"It was Mirror. She looked just like me," Rachael replied.

"She knows who you are, Dana," Rachael informed her, looking straight into Dana's eyes. "She knows your name."

"That's who was at the house," Justin suddenly realized, looking at Dana. "She was calling you out to play the game. It was Mirror."

"I hate you!" Dana suddenly yelled out in anger, looking upwards but nowhere in particular. "Do you hear me bitch?!" she continued. "I HATE YOU!"

"That's probably not a good idea," Justin advised.

"I swear to God, if it's the last thing I do I'm going to send you straight back to hell where you belong!" Dana screamed at the top of her lungs.

"Alright, enough," Justin said, grabbing Dana by the shoulders, trying to calm her down.

"Just get that game out of here," Rachael demanded. "That's all I ask."

"I gotta call Jenny," Dana interjected, still emotional, reaching once again for her phone.

"I'm going to bring her upstairs," Justin said. "Are you okay to walk?" he asked Rachael.

"Jenny, yeah it's me…Dana," she said into her phone as Rachael assured Justin she was fine.

"What the hell is going on?!" Jenny asked nervously. "It's been forever. I've been pacing the floor nervous as shit."

"It knows who I am!" Dana began. "Mirror," she corrected herself. "She knows my name. She tried to kill my friend!"

"Wait...what!!" Jenny asked, confused and becoming pissed off at the same time. "I told you not to play the game!" Jenny yelled into the phone.

"I didn't play it," Dana defended herself. "I left it here. I was on my way to see you...we were like 2 minutes away before I realized I forgot it, and..."

"Are you serious?!!" Jenny asked in disbelief. "You forgot it?"

"I know. I fucked up," Dana admitted.

"I'll say," Jenny agreed, reaching for her cigarette pack to calm her now rattled nerves.

"Don't make me feel worse than I already do," Dana pleaded.

"Well, what do you want me to say?" Jenny asked, taking a drag off her now lit cigarette. "I told you...I warned you this was serious shit!"

"I know. I know," Dana admitted, not coming up with anything else to say.

"Is she okay...your friend?" Jenny asked.

"I think so, yes," Dana answered, watching Justin help Rachael up the stairs.

"She's lucky," Jenny said bluntly.

"The power went out," Dana explained. "It turned the game off before Mirror could kill her."

"So the power is still off?" Jenny asked, assuming.

"Yes," Dana confirmed. "It's like pitch dark down here."

"Dana...the game is still in play mode!" Jenny cried. "If the power comes back on, the game will resume and you won't be able to stop it!"

"Shit!" Dana yelled, dropping her phone and grabbing the flashlight, immediately running to the entertainment center to unplug the game. "It's unplugged," Dana said, back again to her phone.

"Get that game out of there," Jenny demanded. "And bring it here... tonight!"

"I'm so exhausted," Dana admitted. "I just can't. It's unplugged. It's fine."

"You said she knew your name, right?" Jenny asked.

"Yes," Dana confirmed "Well, that's what Rachael said."

"Its power is growing stronger," Jenny declared. "I don't know how or why, but you're not safe and that game is connected"

"I think the house is connected too," Dana added and agreed with what Jenny had said.

"So get it out of there," Jenny reiterated.

"Alright, fine," Dana submitted. "But I seriously need to take a shower first. You have no idea what I've been through today."

"Oh, I have an idea, but that's okay," Jenny agreed. "Just get it here tonight."

With that Dana ended her conversation and made her way upstairs. David was waiting to greet her.

"Are you okay?" Dana asked, kneeling down to his height to hug him.

"Yeah, I'm fine," David answered. "It was just a stupid storm. But when the lights went out, I hid under the bed."

"Oh you did, did you?" Dana asked, managing a smile.

"Yeah, that's where I always go when there's monsters," he stated.

"David, did you see any monsters?" Dana asked, as her smile instantly left her face.

"No, but I thought I heard one," he said. "It was loud, and I heard Rachael screaming. But then I know she was playing a game, because she always screams at games she sucks at."

"Alright...I think that will do," Justin said, ending David's story knowing this would further upset both Rachael and Dana.

"And you shouldn't be using that word," Rachael put in, sitting on a chair in the kitchen trying to nurse a bottle of water and holding a rag full of ice on her cheek.

"Yes, it's not very polite," Dana agreed.

"I'm sorry," David apologized. "Rachael tripped in the dark and hurt her face," he said to Dana.

"Yes, I know"'" Dana said looking at David and realizing the story Justin must have come up with.

"Hey, I found some of these candle jars in the other room and some matches," Justin said, rejoining them.

"They're my mom's Yankee candles. She'll kill us," Dana acknowledged.

"Well, considering the circumstances…" Justin pointed out. "And we only have one flashlight," he added, holding up the flashlight as if to demonstrate the fact.

"Alright, give me one," Dana agreed.

"Pineapple, strawberry, or…" Justin paused to read the label on the last one with the flashlight. "Caramel cream," he finished.

Dana grabbed the caramel cream, not that she really cared but why not.

"I'm taking a shower," Dana stated, as she struck a match to light the candle jar, stuffing the remaining pack in her front pocket. "After that I'm going to see Jenny, but I want you to stay with Rachael and David," Dana said to Justin walking away.

"Alright," Justin agreed.

Dana made her way slowly to the upstairs bathroom holding the candle jar, which offered very little help against the darkness, other than to cast eerie looking shadows on the hallway walls. Nonetheless she found the bathroom, based more on memory than anything else. Placing the jar, the book of matches and her cell phone on the sink top, Dana got undressed and carefully removed what were already soaking wet bandages from her legs. In the small room the candle did much better by means of emitting light, but not good enough to clearly see her wounds. That would have to wait for some other time.

"Finally!" she exhaled, feeling elated by the soothing pulse of hot water shooting from the shower head above her. "I think I could stay in here for an hour," she thought to herself, opening up her body wash that shortly after filled the room with the fresh scent of Lilac. It was the first time during the entire day she could clear her head, relax, and feel a sense of normality. But that normality would soon be short-lived.

"Shit," she said out loud, as the light from the candle suddenly extinguished. "Oh, that's just great," she said again out loud, trying to rinse the body wash off her body in the dark. Doing that the best she could, Dana reached aimlessly in the dark towards the direction in which she had placed the towel. With the door closed and the candle light gone, she literally couldn't see her hand in front of her face. After several attempts she did manage to locate it. Drying herself off and taking baby steps to feel her way around the room, she arrived with her hands on the sink top and found the book of matches. Quickly bringing one to life, she relit the candle and immediately saw something written on the fogged up mirror in front of her.

Good luck with that, Dana read to herself with a chill running down her spine. Dana took her hand and wiped off the mirror, waiting a few seconds before it fogged up again.

'Good luck with what?" Dana asked the mirror.

"Sending me back to hell," it answered.

Normally any other person would run away as fast as they could, but at some point fear turns to anger and defense takes over.

"Why are you here?" Dana asked.

"You left the door open," it answered.

"What door?" she asked. "I don't understand." But there was no reply. "Who are you?" Dana tried another question.

"You're looking at her," it answered, referring to her reflection in the mirror.

"We're not playing the game!" Dana exclaimed. "You're not Mirror. Mirror is just a stupid character someone made up."

No reply.

"And by the way," Dana continued. "I hope you enjoyed playing it, because I'm going to destroy it!"

Just then both lights flanking the left and right side of the mirror suddenly lit up, getting brighter and brighter until it was almost blinding and then exploded with a quick burst of sparks.

"Temper, temper," Dana taunted, after jumping slightly from the explosion and the flying shards of glass. "I'll find out who you really are," she went on feeling emboldened. "And I'll find a way to send you back. You're the one that's going to need good luck with that," she pushed.

That was more than enough to send Mirror into a fit of rage. The skeleton face of Elizabeth with her glowing blue eyes appeared in the mirror, letting out an ear-piercing scream before shattering the glass into hundreds of pieces and sending them crashing into the sink below.

9

A HISTORY LESSON

"The past can reveal many things
better left to lay at rest."

Later that evening…

"I'm here to see Jenny Aldren," Dana said to the receptionist, while holding the game box and laptop under her arm.

"I remember you," the black lady with glasses said, handing her a clipboard and pen to sign in with. "I'm sorry, you can't bring that in," she stated pointing to the game box. "No cords are allowed."

"Alright," Dana said, setting the box on the counter. "Do you have a paperclip I can use?" Using the paperclip the lady handed her, Dana pressed the forced eject button to eject the game. She couldn't risk plugging it in here and possibly starting the game. "I'll get it when I come back," Dana said, stuffing the game in her pocket and picking up her laptop. "Room 413, right?"

"Third floor and down the hallway, yes," the woman answered.

Dana arrived shortly at Jenny's room and knocked on the door.

"It's me, Dana," she said.

"Dana!" Jenny said cheerfully as she opened it, immediately noticing

91

the cuts across Dan's exposed legs. "What the hell happened to your legs?"

"It's a long story," Dana answered, walking in with her laptop.

"Good thing this is fully charged," she said, setting it on the table next to Jenny's cigarettes and ashtray. "They won't let you bring cords in here."

"Yeah, they're afraid we might try hanging ourselves or some shit like that," Jenny informed her. "Want a water?"

"Yeah, sure," Dana said.

"Alright, so tell me what's going on," Jenny said, after reaching for two bottled waters from a hotel-like refrigerator and handing Dana one. "Don't leave out a single detail."

Dana went on for probably 30 minutes explaining everything that had happened up to the encounter she had with the mirror.

"So the house is definitely haunted, and the game is connected in some way. But how?" Jenny asked. "And why?"

"And how can it communicate with us outside of the game?" Dana asked as well.

"I found someone that might be able to help," Jenny said, pulling out her phone. "I saved the link," she said as she turned it on.

"How do you power your phone by the way?" Dana asked. "I mean since you can't have cords."

"Oh, we have these," Jenny said, reaching for her charger plugged into the wall behind where she was sitting. "See?" she asked, showing Dana. "Only 8 inches long. Not enough to hang yourself," Jenny demonstrated trying to fit it around her neck jokingly.

"That's funny," Dana laughed.

"So…oh, here it is," Jenny said, showing the link to Dana.

"World renowned parapsychologist Charles Stattmore," Dana read out loud. "He's from England," she acknowledged, reading more.

"London," Jenny agreed. "Anyway, I spoke with him and…"

"You talked to him?" Dana asked, becoming excited.

"Yeah I talked to him, and he said he would do a video chat with us," Jenny finished.

"When?" Dana asked anxiously.

"Well, probably now," Jenny answered. "It's what 7 or 8 in the morning their time?"

"Let me see the link again," Dana said, opening up her laptop and typing it in as Jenny held the phone for her to see.

Moments later, they were fortunate enough to be video chatting with a man they were hoping could provide some answers.

"I see," Charles said with a strong English accent, after Dana had updated him with the information Jenny had not known previously. "Well," he began, taking off his glasses to wipe his eyes and then scratching his thick gray beard. "I think it's rather quite obvious what's going on here actually. You said you played this game on Hallows Eve, correct?"

"Halloween, yes," Jenny confirmed.

"No, Hallows Eve," Charles corrected her. "Halloween is an American 21st century watered down version, where children walk the streets in ridiculous costumes begging for candy. Hallows Eve, on the other hand, dates back to the ancient Celts. They believed that on that day and only on that day, the walls between the Other world…or Underworld if you will…are thinned."

"Meaning what?" Jenny asked, not sure.

"Meaning," he continued, "It's not easy for a spirit to crossover into the living. The barrier is too strong. But on this particular night…if there's a clear path…it can be done."

"What do you mean by a clear path?" Dana asked.

"Well, that's where the game fits into all of this," he explained. "What is also believed is that Hallows Eve is the one night, once a year, where the dead are allowed to return to their home. Well, if it still exists that is. The problem is spirits are lost or sometimes trapped. They need a direction, a portal, a door so to speak that they can come through."

"You left the door open," Dana jumped in. "That's what she meant," she said, referring to what Mirror had told her.

"Yes, exactly," Charles agreed. "By playing that game on that particular night…and in that house…you basically opened up the front door to the other side."

"But I still don't understand," Jenny said confused. "How could playing that game open a door?"

"Well, any other type of game wouldn't have," he began to answer. "But VR, virtual reality, is something quite different. Reality is what we perceive it to be. Some people claim dreams are real and a form of reality. That's why it tricks our minds, makes our brains think we're really experiencing something, an affect, a movement, a rollercoaster ride for example. It's another dimension, a virtual dimension, a form of reality. When you turned that game on, it became the dimension in which they could enter. They really don't know the difference."

"Unbelievable," Jenny said, speaking through a cigarette she had just lit. "How the hell would we have ever known that?"

"Well, most people wouldn't have," Charles answered.

"Wait, but…so the characters in the game are spirits, right?" Dana asked. "But who are they really?"

"Well, I'm not so certain that they are spirits in the plural sense," Charles said. "More than likely one spirit, occupying and controlling them all."

"Occupying them?" Jenny asked.

"Yes," Charles answered. "Well, more of a possession actually. You see, evil spirits…and by the way I believe this is one in your case…can have the power to possess a person, but it's not easy. A person can fight back, depending on how strong their soul is and how much they believe in God. But a computer generated character has no soul, no willpower to fight back. They're just algorithms and computer codes. To a spirit it's a piece of cake to possess."

"So, if we destroy the game, we destroy the characters they...or it... possessed?" Jenny asked in bewilderment.

"If you destroy the game, you close the door. That much is certain," Charles answered. "But it will be trapped in that house with no way out, no path back to the other world."

"So...that works for me," Dana said almost laughing.

"No, I don't think you get the big proverbial picture," Charles said. "It has already possessed the characters in the game and all the powers or physical attributes the software intended it to have. Destroying the game shuts the door, but not what it has become. And it will only grow stronger."

"So you're telling me now that this thing...this bitch...and I believe she is female by the way, can pick or choose the characters in the game she wants and then exist in our world?" Dana asked.

"Not physically," Charles stated. "It can only do that if you play the game, if you're in its reality...for now. Look, I'll make this as simple as I can. Entities, or souls, want what you have. They want to be alive, which they can't be anymore. They're jealous, but there are ways to cheat death, ways to interact in our world if the circumstances permit. My advice to you is to do some research on that house. Chances are something went terribly wrong there. Whatever came home is not friendly and uses the characters in the game as her defense."

"You said (her)," Dana noted.

"Duly noted," Charles observed. "Yes, I believe this entity is female as well."

"But she appeared in the mirror," Dana stated. "And we weren't playing it, so how is that possible? She was communicating with me."

"Mirrors are believed by many to be portals to the spirit realm," Charles explained. "They can't crossover through them, but they can speak through them. As I said, the longer it has the opportunity to at least partially exist in our world, the more confidence it will gain and the more strength it will acquire. Anything is possible."

"So that's it?" Jenny asked, a little disappointed.

"I'm afraid so, yes," Charles answered. "Do some research. Find out what happened in that house and get back to me. There might be something we can use to our advantage."

One hour later…

"You're not going to believe this!" Dana said with excitement, spinning her laptop around for Jenny to see.

"Somebody actually wrote a book about this house," she continued.

"Are you sure?" Jenny asked with tired eyes, trying to see what the excitement was about.

"The true story of Elizabeth Franklin, a witch's tale," Dana read out loud.

"A witch's tale?" Jenny asked, not impressed. "Dana, I'm really tired and it's almost like what…2 in the morning?" Jenny said, yawning.

"Well, do you have anything else you can do around here?" Dana asked, a little annoyed.

"Yeah, it's called sleep," Jenny answered.

"Then sleep," Dana responded. "I mean I'm tired too, but I'm onto something."

"I'm actually surprised they didn't kick you out of here by now," Jenny said, getting up from her chair to take comfort in the blanket her bed offered her not too far away.

"This is interesting," Dana said, as she began to read the online book.

"Uh huh," Jenny agreed, making herself comfortable and pulling the blankets around her body.

"You should notice there's only one bed here," she said. "That's the one I'm lying in and trust me, that chair is not comfortable."

"Nighty, night," Dana acknowledged as she began to read.

...1861...

It was 1861. The Civil War had just begun only a few months ago, but Elizabeth Franklin didn't care too much about it. There was no reason to. She had her own agenda. She was raised as a witch, a heretic as the English liked to call them. Well, she never felt much difference between herself and other girls her age at the time, not until she grew older. But there were differences. Religion for instance. Certain pagan holidays her mother or grandmother would press on her for a matter of importance that no one else in her village would pay mind to. Her father had passed away long before she could remember. He died of an influenza plague that was going around. Influenza that she was certain her mother could have healed had she only had the desire to use her skills as a witch. But for whatever reason she chose not to. Knowing that, learning that from her grandmother as a child, drew a wedge between her and her mother. A wedge that sealed their relationship as a failure, denying any chance of ever having that special mother/daughter bond. No, that relationship belonged to her and her grandmother, and now she was dying as well. Elizabeth watched helplessly as she slowly withered away and begrudged the fact that once again her mother would do nothing. She argued with her mother to save her, to cheat death and relinquish the pain and suffering her grandmother was enduring. But just as with her father, her mother refused, preaching to her that using that kind of power has consequences. Consequences you don't understand and that you need not know. Elizabeth was 23.

"You must promise me child that you will keep up with your witchcraft studies," her grandmother said, as she lay in bed holding Elizabeth's hand while she kneeled down beside her.

"I promise grandmother," she replied.

"Your mother does not agree with the ways in which I teach you," her grandmother stated.

"You teach me strength," Elizabeth stated. "You teach me the power of witchcraft. She teaches me only how not to use it."

"Indeed," her grandmother agreed. "And one day you will be a most powerful witch."

"Will I be immortal?" Elizabeth asked.

"Immortality is a matter of perception," she answered. "Your spirit will live forever, only your body will depart."

"I want to walk amongst the living forever," Elizabeth declared.

"That is a power only few possess," her grandmother stated.

"I see no writing that forbids me of such power!" Elizabeth argued, becoming angry.

"It requires an agreement from the underworld," her grandmother tried to explain. "This is what your mother has tried to hide from you. Perhaps she has seen this quest for immortality in your eyes."

"She sees only what she wants to see," Elizabeth replied. "Soon she will see the sacred dagger through her heart!"

"Only upon my death can I pass the dagger and its powers to your keeping," her grandmother informed her.

"I am aware," Elizabeth concurred.

"You must not allow word of this murder to be heard, understood?" her grandmother asked. "It is a violation of the Witches' Code," she went on. "Your mother stands in the way of your quest, of this I concur, but beware or you will suffer greatly."

"She will die upon my hands and the dagger of which they will be wrapped around," Elizabeth stood her ground.

"Yes, I can foresee it," her grandmother said, closing her eyes and smiling. "You will gain tremendous power. It must be done the eve of my death. I will pass tomorrow on the witching hour."

"I will see you no more?" Elizabeth asked, concerned and beginning to cry.

"Not in this world," she answered, opening her tired eyes.

"What of this agreement with the underworld?" Elizabeth asked.

"Can I make such an agreement?"

"Once you kill your mother, you will welcome evil into your soul," her grandmother answered. "Only after that will you have the power to bargain with them."

"And then what?" Elizabeth asked.

"Elizabeth, you are much too ambitious and overconfident," her grandmother replied.

"It is your teachings," she returned.

"What I have taught you is how to become a powerful witch!" her grandmother said, becoming slightly annoyed. "There are witches 100 years old that have sought what you do. You wish to steal your power. That is fine. I have already given you my blessing upon that matter… (coughing)…but as I have warned you, if you are not careful you will have nothing from which you can bargain."

"You warn me of consequences but yet you agree with what must be done," Elizabeth shouted, standing up. "You tell me I must have power to bargain with, but then you tell me that power has a price. You are talking to me in riddles!"

"I am growing tired child," she stated, closing her eyes. "You will understand. Withdraw the sacred dagger from the cellar and bring it to me in the morning."

"Yes, grandmother," Elizabeth said, leaning over to kiss her on the forehead and pulling her blankets up to keep her warm. "Goodnight," she said, blowing out the candle by her bedside.

…moments later…

"You were with your grandmother I presume," Mary Franklin said, seeing Elizabeth walk into the kitchen as she placed a fresh baked pie onto a hot plate.

"She is dying, in case you haven't noticed," Elizabeth replied scornfully.

"And I guess you blame me for that," her mother said, placing the hot plate and pie into the waiting red-hot embers of the fireplace.

"I blame you for a lot of things, but it makes no difference at this point," Elizabeth concurred, taking her place at a long wooden table and reaching for a basket full of fresh fruit.

"She is my mother," Mary stated, turning around from her work at the fireplace to address her and wiping her hands on her apron. "Why do you think I hate her so?"

"It is not that I think you hate her," Elizabeth replied. "But rather you don't understand her...or me for that matter."

"She teaches you evil," her mother shot back.

"And what do you teach me?" Elizabeth asked, picking up an apple and examining it before taking a bite.

"I teach you witchcraft, but we don't live in the 16th century," her mother professed.

"We were more powerful then," Elizabeth stated, turning a rotten side of the apple over to take another bite.

"And we were burned at the stake," her mother rebutted. "Elizabeth, times are different. You can't live in the past and believe in things that were written so long ago."

"But they were true," Elizabeth defended.

"Okay," Mary said, pulling up a chair to sit down. "What do you want? I mean really...what is it I am doing wrong that upsets you so much?"

"You are weak, Mother," Elizabeth answered, throwing what was left of her apple into a nearby basket. "You have lost the dignity of what it means to be a witch."

"I am trying to raise a daughter, not a witch!" her mother yelled, standing up from her chair while slamming her fist on the table.

"I am your daughter by birthright only," Elizabeth said, trying to find a better apple from the basket. "And you are gravely mistaken," she added, picking one up, "if you think I am not a witch."

"Your grandmother has turned you against me. I know that," her mother said. "But I love you regardless."

"And did you love my father?" Elizabeth asked.

"Of course I did," Mary replied.

"Then why didn't you save him?" Elizabeth asked.

"Elizabeth it's not that easy," her mother answered.

"It is that easy!" she yelled. "You're just a coward!"

"And what, make a deal with the devil?" her mother rebutted. "Is that what you would have wanted?"

"Power knows no boundaries," Elizabeth stated.

"That's your grandmother talking," her mother said. "It's a shame she put such thoughts in your head."

"What happened to you mother?" Elizabeth asked, staring at her apple.

"When I was your age, I was just like you are now," her mother began, sitting back down in the chair. "We were still living in England then, as you know. Anyway, we were at an art gallery. I don't remember exactly where... and I saw a painting of Griselda."

"She was a great witch. A legend actually," Elizabeth noted.

"She was considered a Goddess of the underworld Elizabeth," her mother interjected. "I could see the evil in her eyes. I thought to myself that she was some mother's daughter, that when she was just a child she was so pure and full of innocence. Who she became in the painting was not who she was, and not by her choosing. Somebody made her that way. I swore that day that I would not raise my daughter in such a way as to become a pawn to Satan."

"I see," Elizabeth said. "So you purposely held me back and taught me things only a foolish mortal would deem of importance."

"Is the web your grandmother weaved in your mind so thick now that you consider yourself other than a mortal?" her mother asked. "We are all mortal human beings Elizabeth. Only Gods and Goddesses are above us."

"I will be a Goddess!" Elizabeth yelled, standing up and having enough of the conversation. "You should renounce your faith as a witch," she added, walking away and turning around to toss the apple for her mother to catch. "You don't deserve to be called as such."

Mary remained at the table for several minutes after Elizabeth walked out. Normally the smell now permeating the room of apple pie baking would enlighten her mood, but instead she was oblivious to it altogether. She sat with her head buried between her arms weeping. She had failed. Her daughter's hatred had turned her heart to stone, and her mother had helped to do it.

Elizabeth ascended the grand foyer staircase to the hallway above, stopping by to check on her grandmother and was content that she was sleeping. She made her way to her bedroom and closed the door behind her. In the morning she would go to the cellar and retrieve the sacred dagger, but for now the hour was getting late and she felt the need to rest. Slipping into her nightgown, she was about to pull the blankets down from her bed when a knock came from her door.

"Yes?" she asked, walking towards it.

"Robert, ma'am," he replied from the other side.

"What are you doing up here in these quarters at this hour?" she asked, annoyed and opening the door.

"Sorry ma'am," he replied, holding a plate of freshly baked apple pie. "Mrs. Franklin told me I oughta bring this to you."

"Tell her to choke on it," she said, tightening the nightgown around her bosom. "And I don't want you up here. Is that understood?"

"Yes ma'am," he answered. "I know it's late but…"

"I don't mean just at this hour. I mean at any hour," she interrupted. "It is not appropriate and this house is not yours to roam about in as you please. Oh, just give me that," she said, grabbing the plate out of his hand forcefully and almost spilling the pie and fork to the floor.

Robert stood there wide eyed in disbelief of her behavior. She had never taken a liking to him, he knew that, but only within the last few years had her hate grown stronger towards not just him but everything in general. It was hard to watch and even harder to remain silent about.

"Well, don't just stand there staring at me," Elizabeth said. "Or should I just close the door in your face?"

"Goodnight ma'am," Robert simply returned and walked away.

10

THE WITCHING HOUR

"The witching hour calls upon thee,
Take that which you seek,
Regret nothing and rejoice in your powers,
Those beneath you are feeble and weak."

...the following morning...

"How are you grandmother?" Elizabeth asked, kneeling once more beside her bed.

"Do you have the dagger?" she replied with her eyes closed.

"Yes, right here," Elizabeth answered, pulling it out from within her dress.

"Give it to me," her grandmother said, reaching out her hand.

Elizabeth placed the dagger into the palm of her hand, realizing the time had come for her to pass.

"Give me your hand," her grandmother said, wrapping her fingers around the handle and opening her eyes.

Elizabeth did as she asked, while her grandmother grabbed her wrist with one hand and ran the razor-sharp blade across her palm with the other. It was a much deeper cut than she had expected, and she couldn't help but flinch from the pain.

"Your wound will heal child," her grandmother stated noticing. "Now take the dagger."

Elizabeth grabbed it from her and held it, feeling her opened gash press against the handle.

"Your blood and this dagger are now one and the same," her grandmother began. "What was once mine and all of the powers it possesses belongs to you. Use it wisely."

"Thank you grandmother," Elizabeth said, leaning over to kiss her forehead.

"The witching hour will soon be upon you," her grandmother reminded her.

"I am ready," Elizabeth acknowledged.

"Watch Robert carefully," she warned. "He has prying eyes."

"Yes," Elizabeth agreed.

"I hope you find that which you seek my dear Elizabeth," her grandmother said, closing her eyes. "I have done all I can do for you in this world."

"Please don't go!" Elizabeth exclaimed, as tears began to run down her face. "You are all that I have."

"Not entirely," she said, as the last gasp of air escaped from her lungs.

"What do you mean?" Elizabeth asked. "Grandmother, what do you mean?"

But it was too late for answers. Her grandmother was dead.

...the witching hour...

It was almost an hour after midnight, the witching hour. Elizabeth had placed a cloak over her grandmother's body and surrounded her with candles. For a better part of the day, she had stayed in the room with her, leaving only once when her mother came in to pay her respects. And now the time had come. Elizabeth quietly closed the bedroom door behind her and stepped out into the hallway, carrying the dagger in her blood soaked bandaged hand. Her mother's room was at the far end, and her careful steps against the creaking hardwood floor made the distance she had to walk seem like an eternity. Moments later she found herself standing at the side of her mother's bed. She was sleeping soundly and lying flat on her back.

"Pity you couldn't have been more like grandmother," Elizabeth said out loud, as she raised the dagger in the air. She paused but only for a second or two and then drove the knife down with all her might deep into her mother's heart. The energy that rushed through her body from the dagger stuck in her mother's chest and her hand still grasping the handle was almost overwhelming, filling the room with a bluish aura.

"What have you done?!" her mother cried out, as blood from her internal injuries began to run from her mouth. "You have conjured up the devil himself!" she gasped from her last breath.

"You chose not to use your power!" Elizabeth snarled, pushing even harder on the knife as the electrical charges began shooting from her mother's dead body and into hers. "But I will most certainly use mine," she declared, as her face transformed momentarily from an astonishingly beautiful young woman to that of a skeleton, forever changing her once brown eyes to a bright and glowing sapphire blue.

"There will be a price to pay," her mother's spirit spoke from inside the room.

"A price for what?" Elizabeth asked, pulling out the bloody knife as her mother's body turned into a pile of ash.

"For the power you now possess but don't deserve," her mother's spirit answered from inside the room. "Goodbye Elizabeth," she said, as the blue aura in the room slowly dissipated and then vanished.

"I owe a price to nobody!" Elizabeth screamed out from once again a skeleton's mouth. "Do you hear me mother?!" she screamed in a fit of rage, her blue eyes glowing brighter. "NOBODY!"

But there was no reply as silence fell upon her.

...the next morning...

"Morning ma'am," Robert said, carrying a pile of fresh split logs twice the size an average man could handle into the kitchen to place on the fireplace hearth.

"It is not necessary to do anymore work around here" she stated, turning around to address him with a cup of tea in her hand and wearing a black dress, suited for mourning. "I am replacing you."

"Ma'am?" he asked, setting the logs down.

"I am selling you," she rephrased. "to the Jackson plantation."

"Ma'am, but why?" he asked concerned.

"My mother passed away last night," Elizabeth began to explain.

Robert pretended the best he could to contort his facial expression into that of shock, not knowing for certain if it was believable or not, but he knew Mary Franklin was dead. He had seen Elizabeth leave her room holding the bloody dagger. It was a cold night and Robert had left his quarters to stoke the kitchen fireplace one last time before settling in. But of the five bedrooms occupying the second floor, Mary's was the only one directly adjacent to the grand staircase. Had it not been for the strange blue light bleeding out from beneath her door and brightening the otherwise darkened foyer below, he would have returned to his room. But it was rather peculiar, so he decided to have a look. It was then that he saw Elizabeth.

"I know it saddens you," Elizabeth went on. "Apparently the grief of grandmother passing was too much for her heart. Well, that is the opinion of the doctor."

"May I see her ma'am?" Robert asked. "Be nice to pay my respects."

"Absolutely not," she responded. "It is not the place of a slave to be involved in such personal matters. She will be buried next to grandmother. You may visit her grave whenever the feeling to do so becomes you."

"Thank you ma'am," Robert said.

"So you see Robert, I will be in charge of this plantation now," she stated. "And I believe your fondness towards me or shall I say a lack thereof will interfere with your duties here."

"No...no ma'am, not at all," he returned. "I mean...well, I mean I have no disregard for you ma'am."

"Oh please, don't flatter me with a mouthful of lies," Elizabeth said.

"I beg you ma'am," he pleaded, removing his farm hat as a courtesy. "This place...well this place is my home. It's all I got."

"Well, I can't say I blame you for feeling that way," she said taking a sip of her tea and thinking for a moment. "Very well, you may stay here."

"Thank you ma'am!" Robert exclaimed with a smile. "I'm much obliged."

"Yes, well don't abuse my generosity," she returned. "I hear the Jacksons beat and whip their slaves quite frequently over there, and I won't hesitate to sell you to them."

"You be the boss now ma'am," Robert said.

"Indeed," Elizabeth agreed, smiling. "Now leave me. I'm in mourning as you know."

"Yes ma'am," he said, placing the farm hat back on his head and leaving the kitchen.

That evening, consumed by what her mother had warned her, Elizabeth lit a torch and opened a large solid wooden door leading to a steep set of stairs and closed it behind her with a loud thud. Flames from the torch danced in the darkness and lit up the stone walls and ceiling, carved out by the backs of countless slaves for the purpose of constructing a hidden weapons and ammunition depot. Carefully descending the steps and using her free hand against the cold stones for balance, she arrived near the bottom and turned with her torch into a small chamber that seemed to go nowhere.

Turning a small stone on the far end brick wall and revealing a keyhole, she removed a set of skeleton keys from her dress pocket, unlocked it, and opened the hidden door. It was here, beneath the ground in this depot the size of a fairly large bedroom, where her grandmother had taught her witchcraft. It was here where her grandmother kept the sacred book of spells and chants. And that is what she had come for. She had an idea what her mother meant about a price to pay, for it was considered treason to steal a witch's power upon death unless it was willfully given. Her grandmother had warned her about that. But to invoke a punishment, a spell had to be read to summon the gatekeepers, and she needed to find it. Opening the thick black book, laying as it always had been on a wooden 16th century Tudor cabinet that had belonged to her grandmother, Elizabeth began turning the yellowed and fragile pages. What she didn't notice from the chamber outside, returned to darkness for lack of her torch, was a pair of white eyes watching her. A pair of eyes belonging to Robert.

Well, Robert wasn't his real name of course. It was given to him by Elizabeth's mother, who favored him amongst all the slaves on the plantation. She had even taught him how to read and write, which was otherwise forbidden. Just last year he was granted the job of master keeper of the mansion, partly because he was very strong and able to do chores most of the other slaves couldn't, but also because he was actually quite handy at fixing things. And despite his physique, he was the kindest and most caring gentleman you could ever meet. This, Elizabeth's mother liked the most. It had broken his heart to see Elizabeth walking out of the room the night before, holding the bloody knife in her hand.

Robert had quietly followed Elizabeth to the chamber and watched as she continued to flip through the pages, pausing occasionally until finally leaning forward to read something. Whatever it was she was looking for, apparently she had found it.

"No one must ever be able to read this" she said out loud to herself, carefully removing the page from the book. Had it not been forbidden she would have simply destroyed it, but that was out of the question.

Robert looked on as Elizabeth slid open a small drawer underneath the bottom of the 16 century cabinet, placed the torn page inside, and closed it. He would return one day when the time was right, when opportunity afforded itself to discover its importance. For now he saw what he needed to see and quietly left.

11

ROBERT'S REVENGE

"Hide your sins or make no mistake,
Your soul will be lost to deception to take."

...One month later...

"What were you doing down there?" Elizabeth asked, watching from across the room as Robert shut the heavy cellar door.

"Nothin ma'am," Robert answered politely. "Just finished bringin down a load of guns," he continued, trying to hide his nervousness. "Colonel Matthews...he...he came by...told me best to hide em' here. Said he got em' from the Yanks ma'am," he went on.

"I see," Elizabeth spoke, walking over to him and stopping directly in front of him.

"Why don't I believe you?" she asked, leaning into his face with her glowing blue eyes upon him.

"I...I got's the paperwork right here ma'am," Robert stuttered quickly, reaching into his pocket to pull out a piece of paper. "See ma'am?" he said, starting to sweat and reading the paper while his hand shook. "15 Enfield Yankee rifles, care of Colonel Matthews," he read. "That's his signature right there," he pointed out.

"It's a shame my mother taught you to read," Elizabeth stated, grabbing the paper from his hands to examine.

"Sorry, ma'am," Robert said. "I…I was just doin what I was told."

"And from now on you'll do as I tell you," she replied, looking back up at him from the paper in her hand. "Do I make myself clear?" she asked, as electricity began to swirl through her eyes.

"Yes ma'am," Robert said trembling.

"The key," she said, as she began walking away and then stopped, turning back around to him.

"Ma'am?" Robert asked.

"Don't patronize me, fool!" she yelled back in his face again. "Give me the key!"

"Oh…yes…yes ma'am," Robert obliged, reaching into his pocket to retrieve the key to the depot and handing it to her open and waiting hand.

"When you awake tomorrow, you will be blind in one eye until you die," she said as she took the key. "That is my curse and that is your punishment. If you wish to see, never go down there again," she coldly informed him.

"Please ma'am I was just…" Robert pleaded.

"Don't push my generosity," Elizabeth interrupted. "Now remove yourself from my sight."

Robert did just that, but he had already read the paper she had hidden in the cabinet. Even if he had only one eye the following morning from which to see from, it was irrelevant. He had committed the words to memory. It was his gift, and soon he would use it. He would avenge her mother's death and rid the evil that she had bestowed upon the house he grew up in. He would bide his time.

That time would come three weeks later.

"Robert," Elizabeth called out as she walked elegantly down a grand spiral staircase, her white satin and lace dress brushing casually against the red carpet. "Robert," she called again.

"Yes ma'am," Robert answered immediately, entering the mansion's foyer and temporarily relieving himself from his duties in the kitchen.

"I will be going into town and then…" she stopped.

"Ma'am?" Robert asked, now standing in front of her.

"Why do you look at me that way?" she asked.

"I mean no disrespect ma'am," he replied.

"Don't lie to me," she returned. "I can see the hatred from your one eye, and I can smell it from your repulsive sweat."

Robert stood at attention in his black housekeeper suit, hands to his side, and said nothing.

"Mind your manners," she advised him. "Lest you have no eyes from which to bestow your hatred."

"Yes ma'am," he said.

"Anyway," she continued, "when I get back I have a chore for you."

"I'd be obliged ma'am," he stated.

"I want you to remove that old cabinet in the cellar depot. It's quite heavy, so you may call upon a slave to help you," Elizabeth ordered.

"But that belonged to your grandmother," Robert spoke, before realizing it was a mistake to do so.

"You truly like to test my patience don't you?" she said, as her blue eyes glowed brighter.

"No ma'am," he answered.

"The only reason you're even still alive is because my mother would have it that way," she snarled, grabbing his neck with one hand. Robert could feel her strength and realized even he could not escape her grasp. "And I don't have much allegiance to her," she informed him, still holding on as her face, for only a brief second, became a skeleton. Robert had never seen her turn like that before and it was horrifying.

"Forgive me ma'am," he spoke, gasping for breath as she released him. "Ma'am…if…if I may say…" he began.

"What? Speak," she said.

"I'm forbidden to go down there," he reminded her.

"I will accompany you, of course," she said. "I'm having it shipped to London. So you will need to bring it to the carriage house," she instructed as she walked away.

"Yes ma'am," he said.

Elizabeth was taking no chances. She had sold the 16th century cabinet to an Englishman she had shared company with, whom owned an antique shop in London. Her only threat was the witches chant laying in its hidden drawer and soon it would be far away from her.

...Several hours later...

This was the moment Robert had been waiting for. He enlisted the help of another slave he knew and instructed him what to do. There would only be one chance. If they failed, it would mean a certain death. Elizabeth had forced him to relinquish his key to the cellar depot, but as master housekeeper he had several others. This she did not know. It was in his pocket ready to use.

"Ready and waiting I see," Elizabeth noted, returning home and seeing both Robert and his companion standing next to the large cellar door.

"Yes ma'am," they both said simultaneously.

"Very well then, let's go about it," she said, as Robert opened the door and reached for the torch on the near wall to light.

"Watch your step ma'am, seein how you be wearin that dress and all," Robert's companion said.

"You see Robert," she began, as she lifted her dress with both hands to avoid tripping on it. "If you were a little more caring like your friend here, perhaps I wouldn't be so hard on you."

"Yes ma'am," Robert said, leading the way down the steep steps and holding the torch. It was almost time. He could feel his heart racing as they approached the hidden door to the depot cellar.

"Steady the torch, so I can see to unlock it Robert," Elizabeth instructed. "You're holding it up too high."

Robert lowered the torch closer to the hidden door and reached in his pocket for his spare key. It was going to have to be quick. Elizabeth opened the depot cellar door and entered the room. No sooner that she did, Robert slammed the door shut behind her, locking her inside the pitch darkness instantly. Most locks could be opened with a skeleton key from both sides, but not this one. She was trapped. "Have you lost your mind?!" Elizabeth yelled out from the opposite side. "Open this door at once!"

"Treason and trickery from a witches tongue, has cast her fate from which it has come," Robert began reciting from memory.

"Noooooo!" she cried out in horror. "Stop!"

"Through death she has cheated the Witches' Code, and holds in her spirit a power forebode," he continued louder.

"Please, I beg you...stop!!" she pleaded, banging on the door.

"Guardians of hell, I summon thee, to vanquish her soul for eternity," he began to yell.

"You must stop before it's too late!" Elizabeth yelled at the top of her voice.

"Restore the order by which we abide, a soul for a soul, an eye for an eye," Robert went on yelling.

"Don't say the last verse. Please, you don't understand!" she pleaded desperately.

"Cast judgment I ask the powers that be, guardians of hell...I SUMMON THEE!" he finished.

"Do you know what you have done!?" she screamed through the door. "Do you?!!!" she yelled hysterically.

Elizabeth turned around in the darkness waiting for what she knew was coming. "There's a price to pay," she could remember her mother's spirit saying. And then they appeared, the four guardians of hell, demons in every sense of appearance, with their eyes rolled back in their heads.

"I disavow my power," Elizabeth said, dropping to her knees. "I willingly relinquish my power to you," she added, remembering the Witches' Code.

"Only through death may a witch willingly relinquish it," the one spoke.

"The power of which you speak was stolen," another one said.

"You of all should have known the consequence," a third one stated.

"I'm only 23. Please I beg you," she pleaded.

"Mercy is not something we can offer," the fourth one answered.

"You have been judged," the first one to speak declared. "Your soul will be condemned to hell."

"Fine," Elizabeth said standing up. Her eyes aflame in blue, radiating across a skeleton's face. "I will return, for hell hath no boundaries," she said with a vengeance, pointing in defiance. "You will not keep me there forever!" she declared with her last words.

12

AN OFFER TO HELP

"Naiveté runs deep in the blood
of those easily seduced"

...back at the mental institution...

"Well, so that's the condensed version," Dana told Jenny the following morning.

"The condensed version," Jenny repeated sarcastically, still laying in her bed with tired eyes. "You've been reading this story to me for like, I don't know, 30 minutes," she pointed out, yawning and slowly getting up from her bed.

"Well, I've actually been up all night reading it," Dana stated.

"Wow!" Jenny exclaimed. "Strange that they didn't kick you out."

"I know, right?" Dana agreed. "So...like can you get coffee around here or what?" Dana asked, curious and in desperate need.

"Of course. Downstairs," Jenny answered. "And breakfast too."

...moments later...

"So, this woman...this witch..." Jenny began asking, taking a bite of an egg sandwich and speaking with a mouth full.

"Elizabeth Franklin," Dana interjected.

"Right, Elizabeth," Jenny concurred, swallowing. "So she killed her mother if I'm getting this right, yes?"

"Correct," Dana answered.

"Alright, so…" Jenny continued, reaching for her cup of coffee and taking a sip. "She was a witch and her mother was a witch and somehow she gets sent to hell, right?" she asked.

"Because she stole her mother's power," Dana explained. "She violated the Witches' Code."

"Oh c'mon!" Jenny exclaimed. "Seriously? It's a book, Dana."

"Take a look at this," Dana asked, pulling out her phone to show Jenny a picture she had downloaded from the book. "That's Elizabeth," she stated, turning the phone in Jenny's direction to view. "It's in black and white but does she look familiar?"

"Oh my God," Jenny said, as she put her hand across her mouth. "She was there. She said we weren't welcome in her house and that we would all die. It's her. It's definitely her," Jenny stated.

"Remember what Professor Charles said?" Dana asked.

"On Hallows Eve it's the one night and only night that the dead can return to their home," Jenny repeated what she had remembered.

"And on that night the game you and your friends were playing opened the door for her," Dana concurred.

"Shit…so she's back," Jenny agreed.

"In some way yes, I think so," Dana answered. "I will return, for hell hath no boundaries," she repeated what she read in the book. "We need to go back to that house."

"We?" Jenny asked. "No, there is no WE here. There's no way I can get out of here!"

"I have an idea about that," Dana said, sipping her cup of coffee and watching for the expression on Jenny's face.

"Don't even think about it Dana," Jenny said, stuffing the last piece of her sandwich in her mouth.

"The police would be looking for me before we even got there," she said, finishing it and wiping her fingers on the napkin in front of her.

"That's the last place they would look," Dana tried to make her case.

"Why? Why, do you need me?" Jenny asked point-blank.

"Because I think we will need to play the game," Dana stated.

"Oh…no way," Jenny returned emphatically. "Are you seriously crazy?"

"Maybe," Dana admitted. "But it might be the only way."

"Only way for what?" Jenny asked. "Look, I get it now. I know why all this crazy shit happened," she said, lighting a cigarette and pausing to speak while she took a drag and exhaled. "But I'm done," she went on. "There's nothing that can change what happened and nothing anybody can do to get me out of here. So, I really don't see the point."

"So you would rather just rot here then?" Dana asked.

"I don't know. I guess me and my friends caused this, right?" Jenny asked. "And they died for it."

"Jenny…" Dana said, placing her hand on her arm to comfort her. "You and your friends had no idea. Elizabeth vowed to return and she found a way. We need to stop her or else your friends will have died in vain."

"So how do we stop her?" Jenny asked. "I mean, please tell me you have a plan."

"Well, I don't know. I think so," Dana said.

"You think so, or you do?" Jenny asked.

"I have a plan, but I don't know…I don't know if it will work," Dana confessed.

"Then I'm out of it," Jenny declared, getting up to walk away.

"Wait, please sit down," Dana begged. "We need to be in that house, somewhere that can trigger her emotions. I'm thinking in the cellar depot."

"For what?" Jenny asked, still irritated.

"Because…Jenny, think about it. She was only 23 years old, and…" Dana tried to continue.

"And you're 18…so?" Jenny pointed out.

"I know, but let me finish," Dana asked.

"Go on," Jenny said, sighing.

"She only wanted to save her father and her grandmother," Dana said. "She was young and full of hatred because of what happened to them."

"She put a knife through her mother's heart, Dana," Jenny reminded her. "And she killed my friends."

"I know," Dana agreed. "But I know in her own heart there's good in her. She pleaded and even offered to relinquish her power not to be sent to hell."

"It's where she belongs," Jenny stated emphatically.

"Do you want to help me or not?!" Dana asked, becoming angry.

"I want to help, but you're not telling me anything," Jenny answered.

"I don't know," Dana agreed to a point. "Maybe I'm just getting too wrapped up in all of this."

"I'd say," Jenny said.

"Okay, fine," Dana admitted, playing with the straw stirrer she still had in her Styrofoam coffee cup. "But what if I'm right?"

"So then you're right," Jenny answered. "I still don't see how that changes a damned thing."

"I guess not," Dana caved in.

"Look Dana," Jenny began, trying to be compassionate herself. "I really appreciate everything. I really do. I mean, in just a short time you have become a good friend of mine, and as you know I don't have any friends now."

"I know," Dana said sadly.

"So, let's just let it go," Jenny suggested.

"Alright," Dana said with a sigh. "I guess I should go."

"Yeah, get some sleep," Jenny concurred. "Hey!" she said, as Dana got up from the table. "Call me tomorrow, don't be a stranger."

"I will for sure," Dana agreed, grabbing her laptop and leaving the cafeteria. But there was no way she was going to let it go. It just wasn't in her nature, and it was on her mind the entire drive home. She was tired, true, but she wanted answers. So when her exit came up on the highway to head home there was a moment of indecision, but only briefly, as she stepped on the gas and headed to Crabtree Road.

"I must be crazy to even think of going back to this house," she thought to herself as she made the turn onto the gravel road, kicking up dust into the dry air. Moments later she could see the familiar mansion towering into the clear blue morning sky. But this time she saw it in a different way. She saw it as she imagined from the book she had read. She imagined how grand it must have looked, just like she imagined when she was a child and stared out of the window of her grandmother's car. She could see Robert tending to the carriages waiting outside to take Elizabeth Franklin to town. And for some reason, she wasn't afraid.

"No, not this time," she said, arriving at the driveway and noticing the thick overgrown bushes that her and Justin fought through before. Taking a pause, she revved up the engine, took aim, and plowed through it, shooting broken stems of straw and weeds into the air and over the hood of her car until she finally came to a rest near the rear entrance of the house. Dana opened her car door, swatting bugs away that she had just stirred up, and entered the still opened door she and Justin had run out of not that long ago. She could see the heavy tapestries she had pulled down from the parlor windows laying where they had fallen on the floor. It was comforting to at least have the sunlight shadowed slightly from the boarded up boards covering them and reflecting upon the dusty floor.

"So where is the kitchen and the entrance to the cellar?" she asked herself, walking cautiously through the parlor to a doorway she hoped would answer her question.

"Oh my God," she jumped, startled as a mouse ran quickly away just in front of her. "This is such a bad idea," she admitted to herself, pressing forward towards the doorway with every creak and crack of the floorboards beneath her feet. Once she passed through, she found herself in the main foyer and was overwhelmed with the grand staircase leading to the second level. It was still beautiful in design, but there was something strange about it, as if the past and present somehow converged. There were parts of the detailed oak railing and carpeted steps that looked like what you would expect from a 150 year old abandoned home. But then there were also parts that looked brand new, like it was just built yesterday.

"Weird," Dana thought to herself looking upwards to observe the windows and tapestry in the two story foyer.

"What is going on here?" she questioned herself, noticing the windows with completely intact glass. "They were all broken out...I know they were."

Suddenly she could feel a chill in the air, almost like how the cold winter air hits you the moment you step outside from your warm heated home.

"Why are you here?" came the irritated voice of Elizabeth.

Dana turned her eyes back to the staircase and saw the clearly identifiable ghost of Elizabeth Franklin, standing at the top step and looking down upon her.

"You were not invited," Elizabeth continued, as she began to descend. It appeared as if she was actually floating, lacking the normal body motions one would expect from a person walking down a set of stairs. She was wearing what looked like an evening gown from the 18th century time period, but it was hard to make out the details considering she was mostly transparent. One thing that stood out though, one thing that was not transparent, were her glowing blue eyes.

"Elizabeth?" Dana asked. "Elizabeth Franklin?" These were the only words she could muster while she stood frozen in her tracks. Part of her was scared to death and the other taken over by sheer curiosity.

Elizabeth abruptly stopped her descent, placing her hand upon the elaborate oak stair handrail. Although there was no wind, her dress and long hair nonetheless seemed to flutter as if there was. Pausing for a moment, she finally spoke. "So, you know who I am," she stated and began once again to descend. "I'm impressed. It's been a long time since I have heard those words spoken from the lips of the living."

"My name is Dana," she said with a lump in her throat, realizing in a moment she would be face to face with Elizabeth's ghost.

"I'm well-aware of who you are child," Elizabeth replied immediately, almost to the bottom of the stairs. "And now I will ask this for the last time, lest you have no ears from which to hear," she stated, now standing directly in front of Dana. "Why are you here?"

"I want to help you," Dana answered immediately, shaking nervously in the presence of Elizabeth's glowing eyes peering into her very soul.

"Help me?" Elizabeth simply repeated pausing briefly. "And why, may I ask, would you presume that I need help? It is you that should be asking this question right now, not I."

Dana tried to maintain her composure. Without even realizing it, she took two steps back to clear some distance between the two of them. The story she had read about her flashed through her mind. She was close enough to see the beauty of what used to be a twenty-three-year-old girl, confused and saddened by the loss of her father and grandmother, and she felt pity for her. It was a character trait of hers that could either be viewed as sympathetic or naïve, depending on a person's perspective. There was something else though, a connection she felt, that for the life of her she could not explain.

"I'm so sorry about your father and grandmother," Dana blurted out what she was thinking. "I know you loved them very much."

That seemed to have an effect on Elizabeth, as the intensity of her glowing blue eyes diminished. "And what do you know of them?" Elizabeth asked calmly.

"I know you wanted your mother to save them, to cheat death," Dana replied.

"Sometimes that for which you want has a price, and they will come for me again," Elizabeth said.

"Who will come for you?" Dana asked.

"The Four Guardians of Hell from whom I have escaped," she answered. "I find it most unsettling, this knowledge you seem to possess of me," she added with a raised eyebrow, leaning in even closer to Dana's face until she swore she could feel a cold chill from her breath.

"I...I read a book about you," Dana hurried a response, reeling back on her toes to maintain her balance.

Elizabeth seemed surprised to learn of a book written about her, withdrawing slightly from her with inquisitive eyes. "Why would there be such a book?"

"I don't know honestly," Dana answered.

"Go on," Elizabeth insisted.

"Ah...about what?" Dana questioned cautiously.

"About this book," Elizabeth pressed.

"Oh...well...I mean it just said that it was your slave...I mean your mother's slave...that summoned the guardians and..." Dana began.

"Robert," Elizabeth sneered from gritted teeth.

"Yes," Dana agreed.

"And this book honored him, I suppose, for doing this," Elizabeth suggested with an angered tone that made Dana more uncomfortable than she already was.

"No, it really didn't. It...it ...well it's just a story so..." Dana tried to reassure her.

"I should have ripped out his tongue!" Elizabeth exclaimed with regret, as the radiant blue in her eyes intensified.

Whatever courage Dana had mustered to have a conversation with a ghost quickly vanished from her face. The idea of having her tongue ripped out was now first and foremost on her mind.

"Yeah, I should…ah…be going now…probably," Dana stuttered, taking a few steps back.

"The gateway is still open," Elizabeth informed her, sensing the anxiety in Dana's voice.

"The door from the game?" Dana surmised.

"Yes," Elizabeth confirmed. "So you wish to help me?"

If there was ever a moment to regret saying something, this was definitely one of them. A part of her wanted to run and hide. The other part, however, wanted answers. She was knee deep in it now anyway, with no way out. "If I can," she squeaked out, swallowing hard.

"Then you must come with me," Elizabeth said, extending her hand out as a bright red orb formed and floated just above it.

"Wait…what is that for?" Dana questioned, seconds before everything in her mind went black.

13

DECEIVED

*"Deception can only be achieved by those
not capable of seeing the truth
tangled in a web of lies."*

Dana woke up from what felt like a huge hangover, pushing herself up from the floor with both hands, white in the face and trying to make sense of what had happened to her. Standing on her wobbly knees, she instinctively reached for something to support her unstable weight. But there was nothing, only a blur of white. She questioned to herself if she was in fact still dreaming before the bulge of her phone, protruding out of her back pocket buzzed, snapping her back to reality. "Shit, it's almost dead," she said out loud after grabbing it to look at it. Dana quickly went to her contacts and scrolled down until she found the name Jenny. "C'mon, c'mon…answer," she said impatiently, as she watched the power level on her phone diminishing to almost 10 percent.

"Dana, what's up?" Jenny finally answered and asked.

"I need your help," Dana stated, panicking. "My phone is dying. I only have like less than 10 percent now."

"What's wrong? Are you okay?" Jenny asked, wrapping a towel around her and holding her phone under her chin. "Sorry, I just got out of the shower."

"I'm at the house," Dana started to say quickly. "I don't know...maybe in the cellar like the book described. I saw Elizabeth...I talked to her..."

"You're at the house?!!" Jenny exclaimed, interrupting.

"Listen, please," Dana begged. "My phone will die any second. She took me somewhere. I'm in a white room. I mean everything is white, but..."

"Oh my God, you're in the game!" Jenny declared, panicking as well.

"It's impossible," Dana stated. "The game is with you."

"Nothing is impossible, but you are definitely in the game," Jenny pointed out.

"She said the door is still open," Dana said. "She said they are coming for her and..."

"Dana?" Jenny asked. "Dana, are you there? Shit!" she yelled, grabbing a cigarette to think and lighting it. Taking a long drag and exhaling, she paced the floor with desperation. There was little, if any, time to waste. Grabbing her phone, she quickly scrolled through her messages, which were surprisingly a lot more than she realized, until finally there it was. Repeating the number to herself several times, she exited her messages and dialed. Of course he didn't recognize her number as he answered with a questioning tone.

"Justin, it's me, Jenny," she said with urgency.

"Oh, hello Jenny," he answered.

"Listen, Dana is in trouble," she stated. "I need you to come get me."

"Wait, what?" he returned, springing up from the couch, forgetting about the movie he was watching as his eyebrows tightened with a look of concern. "Is she okay?"

"Not for long," Jenny admitted. "You have to come get me...now!

She's at the house…the Franklin mansion."

"Slow down," Justin said, rubbing his head nervously. "Why is she at the house, and how do you know she's in trouble?"

"Because she called me," Jenny answered with anxiety. "Elizabeth has her…I don't know…in the house somewhere, but her phone died."

"Who's Elizabeth?" Justin questioned.

"She's a witch. She's the one that killed my friends," Jenny explained.

Why Dana would have even considered going there alone was beyond him. The fact that she did infuriated him as he fumbled with the keys from his pocket and rushed to the front door.

"Alright, I'm going to the house right now," he said.

"But you have to come get me. She needs me," Jenny pleaded.

"It's too far Jenny," Justin reminded her, slamming the door shut behind him in stride to his car. "It would take too long and besides, they're not going to let you leave with me anyway."

"Alright, listen…" Jenny began, with a drag from her cigarette. "Somewhere in that house is a large door that leads down to a cellar, and the…I don't know. There's supposed to be a hidden door in the stone wall. I think that's where she's at…in the hidden room."

"That doesn't sound very encouraging," Justin admitted, starting his car.

"Oh and you're going to have to find a key…a skeleton key…to unlock it," Jenny added.

"Great," Justin said, not feeling very optimistic about it. "I'll call you when I get there," he said, speeding away.

…back at the house…

"I don't get it," Dana said to herself, with both hands on the white walls trying to feel her way around for an exit. "How can a room not have any doors?"

"This is not a room," Elizabeth spoke, appearing behind her.

Dana quickly spun around and saw Elizabeth standing in front of her. "Oh my God, you're real!" Dana exclaimed. "I mean…you're not a ghost…you're…you're…real!"

Elizabeth was wearing her favorite white satin and lace dress. The one she always wore when she would go to town. Her long orange red hair flowed gracefully over the bare portion of her shoulders and her face glowed with the beauty of a young 23-year-old woman. At this moment she was as real as Dana was herself.

"In this reality, yes, I am real," Elizabeth said.

"This reality?" Dana questioned.

"It is a gateway between the living and the dead. One which your friend and hers created," Elizabeth explained.

"You said they will come for you, the four guardians," Dana stated.

"Yes," Elizabeth agreed. "Unless you help me."

"Well, I told you I wanted to help you," Dana reminded her. "But how?"

"You will learn of that soon enough," Elizabeth answered, and then with a blink of an eye, disappeared.

…Jenny…

Jenny knew the consequences of trying to escape from a mental institution, but she was not about to sit here in her room and do nothing when her friend…her only friend…needed her.

"Just wear this dress and put on sunglasses," she could hear Dana saying.

Dana had been purposely wearing the same dress every time she visited Jenny. It was part of her master plan to one day sneak her out. She had bought an identical dress and given it to her as a surprise.

"Why did you waste your money on this?" Jenny could remember herself saying to Dana. "I'm never going to do it."

"Never say never," Jenny said out loud, slipping into the dress and standing in front of the mirror. "Shit, I guess I do look just like her," she admitted with approval as she added the sunglasses for the final touch and stuffed her hands in the dress pockets, feeling something touch the fingers of her right hand. Dana had thought of everything. Inside were two twenty dollar bills paper clipped to a note that read... cab fare.

The plan was to simply walk past the front desk. With any luck the same woman would be there that Dana had come to know fairly well. She would recognize the dress and most likely think nothing of it.

"Well, here goes," Jenny said, closing the door behind her. Jenny made her way down and stood at the end of the hallway leading to the main front entrance and freedom. Her heart was pounding and despite the air-conditioned building, she could feel the sweat forming on her forehead. "You can do this," she thought to herself and began to walk.

Approaching the desk to the right side of the hallway, Jenny briefly glanced over and noticed the familiar face. She was so nervous, she felt as if her knees were going to buckle. "Almost there," she thought, passing the front desk and then...

"Hey!" came the voice from behind the desk. Jenny stopped dead in her tracks and turned around with a lump in her throat.

"Now you know better than that Dana," she said. "Next time don't forget to sign in."

"Sorry," Jenny said, trying to clear her throat.

"Rules are rules hon," the woman said over her half tilted glasses. "You have a good day."

"That's it. I'm out of here," Jenny thought, turning back around with a smile on her face and heading for the front entrance.

...*Justin*...

"Jenny, yeah it's me, Justin," he said into his phone, walking past Dana's mustang he had parked beside. "I'm at the house. Her car is here."

"I'm on my way," Jenny said from the back seat of a cab.

"You got out?" Justin asked, surprised.

"Sure did," Jenny answered proudly. "I should be there in about 30 minutes."

"Alright, I'm going to go in and try to find the cellar door," he said.

"Be careful Justin," Jenny pleaded. "She will know that you're there."

"Yeah, I can't say that I'm happy about that," he admitted.

Justin clicked the button on his car keys to open the trunk and tucked his phone into his back pocket. "Smart girl," he thought, noticing the plowed down weeds and broken off stems covering the hood of her car as he grabbed the flashlight and closed the trunk. "What the hell was she thinking coming here by herself?" he thought, as he headed for the back entrance. Once inside, he knew there was no time to waste. Jenny would be there soon, but waiting for her was not an option. He had to find Dana.

"Dana!" he began to yell out as he quickly went from room to room. "Dana, I'm here. Where are you?" he asked, yelling into the empty house. The floorboards creaked under his every step, giving him a lonely feeling until he finally came across the kitchen and a large oak door that was unmistakable from the description Jenny had given him. It was the cellar door leading to the hidden room and where Dana must be. It had to be. Forgetting that he needed the skeleton key for the hidden room, Justin turned the round and tarnished brass knob and pulled on the door, as the hinges of a more than hundred and fifty year old door fought against him, crying out with a grinding sound. Once open, he shined his flashlight down into the dark and musty smelling stairway.

"Dana!" Justin yelled with an echo. "Are you down there?" he asked again, shining his flashlight against the stone walls sweating with moisture. "Dana?" he asked again, carefully taking a few steps down the steep stone steps, with one hand against the wall, feeling the wet stones on his skin. But something was wrong. He could feel it. It wasn't just the damp smell or the darkness. It was as if something or somebody was watching him. Instinctively he turned around only to find Elizabeth standing on the step above him. Her face was that of a skeleton and her eyes shined in a way that it cast a bluish tint across the darkened walls.

"She can't hear you," she spoke through skeleton teeth, thrusting her face directly into his.

"Ahhhh!" Justin screamed in horror and shock, not prepared for what he saw and losing his balance, dropping his flashlight, and tumbling along with it one step at a time down the steep and hard stones until finally coming to rest at the bottom.

"Fool," Elizabeth simply stated, seeing his motionless body, and disappearing into thin air as the solid oak door slammed shut with a loud thud, sealing Justin in complete darkness.

...Jenny...

"Are you sure this is where you want me to drop you off ma'am?" asked the cab driver, who appeared to be at least eighty years old, with dark skin. "There isn't a lick of anything around here," he spoke with a country farmer's accent.

"It's fine, but yes this is the place," Jenny assured him, reaching into her dress pocket to pull out the only cash she had.

"Well, alright then," the cab driver said, clicking off the meter with a look of concern on his face. "Look ma'am," he continued. "I may be an old fool, but it don't seem right leavin you here...ya know...by yourself and all. You oughta take better care of yourself than comin to a place like this."

"What do you mean a place like this?" Jenny asked with the money in her hand, curious to know. "How much do I owe you?"

"This is the Franklin's old house," the cab driver answered. "Twenty dollars ma'am," he said looking back at her over his seat.

"So you know about them?" she asked as he took her money, interested and not quite ready to leave.

"Of course," he answered. "Ain't too many people that don't…well at least in my time."

"Well, I guess I'm one of the ones that don't," Jenny stated. "Well, other than what my friend told me from a book she read."

"Never read it and don't care to," the driver noted, now turning around facing her with his arm over the seat.

Now she could see him clearly. He was definitely an elderly man, most likely eighty or so, gray hair…well the usual description, except for his right eye, which was glazed over and clearly blind.

"She's evil," he said, staring directly at her with that one blank eye.

"You mean Elizabeth?" Jenny said frankly.

"You're damned right Elizabeth!" he exclaimed through what she noticed were rotten teeth. "She's the one done gave me this dead eye," he said, pointing with emphasis to his right eye.

"Wait," Jenny paused, trying to take all of this in. "Robert?" she asked, afraid of what the answer might be. "Is your name Robert?"

"Yes, ma'am," he replied.

"Oh, shit," Jenny said back, reaching nervously into her pocket for her cigarettes. "But you're…you're dead!" she said, still fumbling with anxiety and finally grabbing the pack.

"Strange things happened when that door opened," Robert began to explain. "I was sent to you. No idea why."

"You mean the door my friends and I opened?" Jenny asked, trying to light her cigarette with shaking hands.

"Don't really know ma'am," Robert answered. "But she's definitely back…Elizabeth I mean,"

"She has my friend," Jenny stated.

"Yes, I know," Robert agreed. "Don't know what I can do to help, but she will use your friend to come into this world. That you can be certain of."

"Where is she? Do you know?" Jenny asked.

"She has her in the cellar, in the weapons depot room," he answered.

"I have to go get her," Jenny said, opening the car door and climbing out.

"You won't be able to save her," Robert yelled, as Jenny slammed the car door shut and began to run towards the house. Jenny made it inside and ran straight to where she remembered the kitchen to be, noticing the large cellar door.

"You will have to try to find a skeleton key," she remembered Dana telling her. "But where?" Jenny said to herself, beginning to frantically pull open the old cabinet drawers one by one.

"I hid the key," Robert spoke.

"Robert?" Jenny asked, turning around in all directions to an empty room.

"It's in the ash pit," his voice spoke again. "In the fireplace."

Jenny ran over to the large brick fireplace and bent to her knees, crawling almost halfway inside. "There's gotta be a cover somewhere," she thought, feeling with her hands over several inches of century old blackened soot until touching metal. "That's it!" she celebrated, placing both hands around the edges and lifting it up, straining against its weight. Setting it aside, she stuck her hand down into the ash filled pit. "I don't feel it," she said, after searching blindly with her fingers for several minutes.

"It's in there," Roberts's voice assured.

"Damn it," Jenny said frustrated, leaning closer and practically laying on her side as she thrust her arm further down into the pit. "I can't reach any further," she said, sifting back and forth through the ash and almost giving up. And then…"Wait. I got it. I think I got it!" she rejoiced, wrapping her hand around what felt like a key and pulling it out. "Oh my God, Dana's going to kill me," she said, standing up with the key and looking down at her soot covered dress. "Alright, let's go," she said, hoping Robert was still with her and walking towards the cellar door. Jenny grabbed the large iron handle and pulled with some resistance to open it. Immediately she could feel the cold damp air rushing past her face, and there seemed to be some kind of light emitting from the bottom. After only a few careful steps down she realized what it was. "Justin!" she yelled. She had become so distracted with Robert and trying to find the key, she had completely forgotten about him.

"You can't help him," Roberts's voice spoke.

"You mean…he's…he's dead?" Jenny asked in terror.

"Yes," Robert replied.

"Oh shit…oh shit," Jenny repeated, continuing down the steps with the aid of Justin's flashlight beam. "I'm so sorry," she said to Justin once she made it to the bottom, leaning down to grab the flashlight off the floor and trying not to look at his mangled and broken body. "So, where's the hidden door?" Jenny asked, shining Justin's flashlight into the dead end corridor.

"At the end," Robert said.

Jenny walked to the end and stood in front of what appeared to be an ordinary stone wall.

"There's a small rock directly in front of you," Robert said.

Jenny put her hand on the wall searching for a small rock. "Here?" she asked, finding one.

"Yes," Robert said. "Pull it open."

Jenny grabbed the rock and pulled on it, opening up a small key hole.

"Open the door," Robert instructed. "You will see me on the other side. Stay close to me."

…Dana…

Dana paced across the white floor in anticipation of what was to come. She wasn't sure if it had been only a minute since she saw Elizabeth or several hours. Time seemed to almost not exist here.

"I am sorry to keep you waiting child," Elizabeth said, suddenly appearing before her.

"No, it's …it's fine," Dana said, momentarily startled.

"Umm…what's the dagger for?" she asked nervously, seeing Elizabeth holding one in her hand.

"You need not worry," Elizabeth told her. "It's not for you. This belonged to my grandmother," Elizabeth continued, holding it in her palm for Dana to observe. "And her grandmother before her and so on."

"It's beautiful," Dana admitted, observing the intricate carvings engraved in the handle and decorated with sapphire stones.

"Yes, it's quite exquisite," Elizabeth agreed, with a tear forming in her eye and rolling down her cheek.

"Why are you crying?" Dana asked sympathetically.

"It was my wish to pass this down as a grandmother, had I lived to bear children," Elizabeth explained.

'I'm so sorry," Dana said, feeling sad for her.

"I have paid a dear price for that which I have done," Elizabeth said.

"I know," Dana agreed solemnly. "What can I do? Please tell me how I can help you."

"You must release my soul, so that I may be at rest with my family," Elizabeth answered, holding out the dagger for Dana to take.

"You want me to kill you?" Dana asked in disbelief. "No, I …I can't," she said, refusing to take it.

"You cannot kill that which does not live Dana," Elizabeth said, still holding out the knife.

"You called me by my name," Dana said, feeling touched.

"Yes," Elizabeth agreed, crying.

Dana reached out to take the knife as tears began to fill her eyes as well.

"It must be in the heart," Elizabeth noted.

Dana held the dagger up in position to make the strike staring directly into Elizabeth's crying eyes and then lowered it.

"I can't do it," Dana said. "I just can't."

"Then my soul will be lost to hell," Elizabeth said.

"Will I see you again?" Dana asked. "I mean, if I do it."

"When your time comes, yes," Elizabeth answered. "I promise."

"Step away from her Dana!" Robert yelled, suddenly appearing from a distance and followed by Jenny.

"Jenny!" Dana yelled out.

"Get away from her," Jenny yelled back, as Robert and her approached.

"You!" Elizabeth sneered with glowing blue eyes towards Robert.

"It's okay. I'm fine," Dana tried to reassure her. "She's not evil, she just needs my help."

"She's trying to trick you," Robert said, grabbing the dagger from Dana's hand instantly.

"This is your grandmother's ritual dagger," Robert said, recognizing it and staring into Elizabeth's eyes with anger. "The same one you used to murder your mother."

"Robert?" Dana asked, suddenly realizing who he was.

"Yes ma'am," Robert said looking over at Dana. "This dagger is only used for sacrifices."

"And whose hand was holding it, fool?" Elizabeth asked.

Roberts's eyes immediately swelled with anger. Too many times in his life she had tormented him with that word.

"My...name...is...Robert!" he exclaimed, turning back to Elizabeth and plunging the knife deep into her heart.

"Nooo!" Dana screamed, eyes wide with horror, as Elizabeth dropped to the floor. "Nooo!" she yelled again, falling to her knees next to her. "Why did you do that?"

"It's okay Dana," Elizabeth said, reaching out to take her hand as the intensity of her blue eyes began to fade.

"Don't touch her!" Robert exclaimed, just as Dana did exactly that, reaching out in return to accept it.

"Dana, listen to him!" Jenny urged, as both Dana and Elizabeth's hands met.

Suddenly Dana began to convulse as blue electricity shot from Elizabeth's hand and into her body, paralyzing her from moving.

"Oh my God! What's happening?" Jenny cried out. "Stop her!"

"It's too late. We can't touch them," Robert informed as they both stood by helpless.

"An eye for an eye, a soul for a soul," Elizabeth began to recite. "I relinquish my powers to whom I behold. Switch our souls so that it may be, from me to her and her to me. This I beseech, my words I implore, so that I may walk amongst the living once more. From the land of the living and the land of the dead, this gateway can be no more. By my sacrifice and by the Witches' Code, I command thee...close the door!"

"You have to get out of here," Robert turned to Jenny quickly.

"I can't leave my friend," Jenny returned, watching Dana crumble to the ground.

"It's not her anymore," Robert said bluntly.

"I don't understand. What's going on?" Jenny asked, confused and becoming a nervous wreck.

"She changed bodies with her," Robert tried to explain. "She tricked her."

"No, I don't believe that," Jenny said, starting to cry.

"Believe what you will, but this gateway will close," Robert said. "And we will both be trapped forever."

"Goodbye my friend," Robert said, touching Jenny's cheek with his hand. "We will meet again." And with that he disappeared, just as if he were never there.

"Dana!" Jenny cried. "I don't know what to do."

"Leave," Dana said from Elizabeth's body, the knife still stuck through her heart and gasping for air to speak.

Jenny kneeled down beside her, noticing Dana's body that Elizabeth had taken over still lying motionless.

"I'm here Dana," Jenny said, grabbing her hand that had almost been burnt to the bone.

"I trusted her. I'm so sorry," Dana said from Elizabeth's lips as her face began to age rapidly.

"No, please don't do this!" Jenny begged to no avail, with tears running down her face.

"Goodbye Jenny," Dana spoke her last words while her hand disintegrated from Jenny's grip into dust, followed by her entire body.

"You must leave," Jenny heard Roberts's voice. "Follow the light."

Jenny stood up and took one last look at Dana's body. She wanted so badly to hug her, but she knew it wasn't Dana anymore.

Suddenly the white walls began to shimmer, as if they were made of water.

"Time to go," Jenny said to herself, beginning to run towards a faint light in the distance. And then the floor beneath her began to look the same, making her feel off balance. The closer she got to the light, the more distorted things became. She was running as fast as she could, but it seemed like she was going in slow motion.

"Now Jenny. Now!" she heard Dana's voice say. "Jump!"

Jenny dove head first into the now blinding light as the place behind her imploded upon itself, ceasing to exist in seconds. Jenny felt the hard stone cellar floor meet her face, taking the wind momentarily from her lungs. Her vision was blurry, but she was certain right before falling unconscious that she could see Elizabeth's glowing blue eyes.

"Hmm," Elizabeth said, stepping over Jenny's body and bending down to pick up her sunglasses lying next to her on the floor.

...moments later...

Elizabeth stepped outside and took a deep breath. She had forgotten what it was like to smell as she drew in the familiar scent of the pine trees still occupying the property as they had a century and a half before. Looking up to the sun, she grabbed the sunglasses hanging between the cleavage of her dress and put them on. There were two cars parked along the side of the house, but she instinctively knew which one was hers. Casually, she walked towards the red GT Mustang, opened the door and climbed in. Reaching for the keys hanging in the ignition, she started the car and brought the radio to life.

Witchy woman roaming in the night
She can stalk your soul with a ravens sight
Run from her, but you cannot hide
From her evil ways and her devils pride
Seeking shelter, but there's none to find
She's gonna get you,
She's gonna get you from behind

"Hahaha!" Elizabeth laughed. "I like it," she said out loud, reaching for the radio knob to turn up the volume. Looking in the rear view mirror to back up, she paused for a moment and took her sunglasses off. "Never trust a witch," she said with a smile to her reflection of glowing blue eyes.

Jenny woke up with her face flat against the stone floor. She was groggy from being unconscious and felt an instant headache the moment she sat up

"Where am I?" she thought for a second, before everything that had happened came back to her. The last thing she could remember was seeing what she thought were Elizabeth's eyes. But then again…maybe not. Looking around she saw the flashlight laying on the floor not too far from her, still on but growing dim. Soon she would be in complete darkness.

"Okay Jenny, get up," she said to herself, standing up. But rather than wait a minute or two to gather her senses, she took a step forward towards the flashlight and instantly lost her balance. "Ahh" she yelled, falling into a wall made of what was now rotted wood boarding. Crashing through it and the cobwebs, she once again landed hard. This time not on the ground, but rather on top of something.

"Great. Just great!" Jenny exclaimed to the darkness. Apparently she was in another hidden room that, for whatever reason, had been boarded shut long ago. "I'm going to get that flashlight if it kills me," she said out loud, getting up from whatever she had landed on with a groan. Staggering and fighting to keep her balance, Jenny climbed over the broken boards she had come through and reached the flashlight. "I'm outta here," she said, holding the dying flashlight in her hand, pulling cobwebs from her face as she began towards the corridor and the steps leading upstairs.

"Wait a second," she thought to herself, stopping and turning around. "There had to have been a reason why that room was boarded up." Jenny walked back to the wall she had fallen through and shined the faint light into it. She wasn't expecting much, but curiosity had gotten the best of her. "Oh shit!" she exclaimed. It was a pile of solid gold bars at least three feet high stacked one on top of each other and four to five bars wide. Obviously it had been hidden during the Civil War and long forgotten.

"Now we're talking!" Jenny smiled, suddenly forgetting the pain she was in.

14

A TRIP TO HELL

"Reach across the divide,
Only in the dream realm
may you achieve that which you seek."

...Two months later...

"Madam, there is a call for you," the waiter said with a Spanish accent, approaching her as his sandals painstakingly dug through the sandy beach.

"I thought I told you that I wasn't accepting any calls," Jenny informed him, as she momentarily pulled the straw to her mouth and took a swallow from her tropical drink.

"She said it's important Madam," the waiter said, now standing in front of her wearing a black uniform one would expect from a very expensive hotel, only with short sleeves and shorts to accommodate the tropical weather.

"She?" Jenny asked.

"Yes, Madam," the waiter said, handing the phone to her.

"It's very important," he added, again with an accent.

"Hello?" Jenny asked, after taking the phone reluctantly.

"So you're alive after all," Elizabeth spoke sarcastically.

"Who is this?" Jenny asked, sitting up from her beach chair and taking another sip through the straw of her drink before setting it down on the table next to her.

"Oh, you don't recognize my voice?" Elizabeth asked.

"Dana?" Jenny asked with an ounce of hope. Well, she had never actually seen Elizabeth come through the gateway, except possibly before she fell unconscious. So, there was no way to really be sure.

"Well, I guess that is a matter of perspective," Elizabeth answered. "But I prefer to be called Elizabeth."

"What do you want?" Jenny asked with a cold hearted voice, not surprised but irritated just the same. "I only took three of your precious gold bars. You killed all of my friends, so I think we're more than even!"

"Oh, it's not money that I am concerned about child," Elizabeth said.

"Don't call me child, you piece of shit!" Jenny yelled into her phone.

"Hmm," Elizabeth paused. "So you see, you are the only one left that truly knows who I am."

"Yeah...and?" Jenny asked, losing her patience.

"And so you must die," Elizabeth answered bluntly.

"Ya know, what the hell is wrong with you?" Jenny asked, as she reached for her pack of cigarettes. "It's not good enough for you that you're walking around in my best friend's body?" she said as she pulled out a cigarette to light and paused..."whom you killed by the way," she said as she lit it.

"She wanted to help me," Elizabeth informed her.

"Oh, don't give me that bullshit!" Jenny yelled, taking a drag and exhaling. "You tricked her. Do you really think I'm that stupid?"

"You're a mortal, so your question is one that deserves no answer," Elizabeth returned.

"Really?" Jenny shot back. "And who are you? A witch that fucked up so bad that you were sent to hell. Where you belong, by the way.

And the only way out was to cheat. You cheated death and took my friends life. In my eyes, that makes you a complete loser!"

"Control your temper," Elizabeth said. "You didn't speak to Dana in such a way."

"You're not Dana!!" Jenny screamed into the phone so loud that she noticed people around her staring.

"I still have all of my powers, so you should mind how you talk to me," Elizabeth shot back.

"But you don't bleed witches blood anymore," Jenny informed her. "You bleed Dana's blood."

Elizabeth paused for a moment. She wasn't sure actually about what Jenny had just told her. It's true, she did exchange her power, but perhaps the blood that flowed through her veins was not hers anymore.

"I will take that into consideration about what to do with you," Elizabeth finally conceded.

"Come and get me," Jenny said, raising her arms to accentuate her emotions.

"Perhaps in time I will," Elizabeth stated.

"And I will be waiting," Jenny answered back.

...*Five years later*...

"So, Halloween is coming," Daniel said, taking a sip of his coffee and setting it down gently on the table.

"Yes, I know," Jenny answered with her back turned to him as she flipped the pancakes over in the skillet. "But do we really have to make a big deal about it?" Jenny asked, turning around and wiping the sweat off of her forehead with the back of her hand.

"Well, I don't know," he answered, reaching for the newspaper. "I just thought it would be nice for Lilliana. She will be five this year and most children her age enjoy trick or treating."

"She's not old enough," Jenny said, not wanting to have this conversation and turning back to the stove.

"Jenny, is there something you're not telling me?" Daniel asked, setting the newspaper back down that he had not even begun to read.

"I hate this time of year!" Jenny exclaimed, reaching for her pack of cigarettes.

"And I thought we agreed you were going to quit that," Daniel stated.

"Yeah, well," Jenny said, lighting her cigarette. "There's things about me you don't know," she confessed, taking a drag and exhaling.

"We've been married for almost 5 years," Daniel said, pulling his chair out from underneath him and standing up. "Maybe it's time you talk to me," he continued, as he approached her to put his arms around her.

"I can't," Jenny said, beginning to cry. "It's…it's nothing…really," she said, trying to convince him and feeling his arms around her.

"Hey, look at me. Look at me," he repeated, as Jenny turned to look into his eyes. "I love you. There is nothing more special in my life than you and Lilliana. But every year when Halloween approaches…it's… it's like I don't even know you."

"Because you don't!" Jenny exclaimed, breaking his embrace and heading for the front screen door with her cigarette in her hand, leaving the pancakes on the hot skillet unattended.

"Jenny, wait!" Daniel said, going to the stove to turn it off and sliding the pancakes onto a dish before they got burnt.

Daniel was ten years older than her, but you wouldn't know it from looking at him. He wore his age quite well. Although he was not particularly a fitness freak, he did keep himself in pretty good shape. She had met him on the beach shortly after she arrived here in Mexico. It seemed like such a long time ago. So much had happened since then, and quite honestly for a while everything seemed fine, great actually. She had fallen in love with a man that made her forget her past and all the pain and anguish she had suffered through. Even the mental institution seemed like a distant lost memory, as if she were never even there. When she became pregnant, she had finally come to peace with all that had happened in her life. It was so hard to let Dana go, but it was time. That was before the nightmares started.

…Later that night…

"Are you okay?" Daniel asked half asleep, as Jenny sat straight up from her bed in a cold sweat, waking him up. "Jesus, it's like…3 in the morning," he said, pausing to look over at the clock sitting on the nightstand next to him.

"I can't help you," Jenny said with glazed over eyes. "There's nothing I can do."

"Jenny!" Daniel exclaimed, sitting up and gently shaking her. "Jenny, wake up."

"I don't understand," Jenny continued in her sleepless state. "Why are you there?"

"Jenny!" Daniel yelled, reaching over to the nightstand and switching on the lamp light. "Wake up honey!" he yelled again, only this time shaking her more vigorously. "You're having a bad dream."

"Get off of me!" Jenny yelled, as she finally woke up.

"What the hell is wrong with you?" Daniel asked, concerned.

"Oh shit, was I dreaming?" Jenny asked, coming to and pushing the blankets away from her with her feet.

"You were having a nightmare," Daniel said exhaustively and rubbing his eyes.

"Where's Lilliana?" Jenny asked, as she slid over to her side of the bed and got up.

"She's in her room," Daniel said. "Obviously…like she always is at this time of night."

"Well, I have to check on her," Jenny replied, still half asleep and stumbling to the bedroom door, foregoing her usual nighttime slippers. Jenny left the bedroom and walked down the short hallway to Lilliana's room. The door was half cracked as it always was. Lilliana insisted upon it when she went to sleep.

"See, she's sound asleep," Daniel said from behind her as Jenny peered in.

Content with seeing her daughter peacefully at rest, she stumbled behind Daniel back to the bed and climbed in, her body still perspiring and in no need of blankets.

"So, what was your nightmare about?" Daniel asked, laying on his back with his arms behind his head and now wide awake.

"It was nothing," Jenny answered bluntly. "I don't know...I don't really remember," she lied.

"You were saying to someone that you can't help them...that there's nothing you can do," Daniel stated. "I remember you saying that."

"Well, I don't remember, okay?!" Jenny shot back at him angrily.

"Okay, okay," Daniel answered, surrendering and pulling the covers over his shoulder, turning on his side away from her.

"Good night," Jenny acknowledged.

"Good night," Daniel yawned, as he reached to switch off the nightstand lamp.

Jenny laid there in the dark staring at a ceiling she could not see. Maybe it really was just a nightmare. Halloween would be in 3 weeks, and she always did feel on edge around this time of year. "That's probably all it is," she thought, trying to convince herself. But despite her efforts to let it go, she couldn't help replaying over and over in her mind what she had dreamed. Dana was in pain. She was in hell and suffering. "Help me Jenny. Please, dear God, help me!" she could hear Dana's voice begging.

"I can't help you Dana," Jenny whispered the words from her lips, as she continued to stare at the darkened ceiling above her. "I wish I could," she added, as a tear rolled down her cheek.

...The following morning...

"Mommy, you didn't pack my lunch," Lilliana said coming into the living room wearing her school clothes.

"Lily honey, today is Sunday," Jenny answered with a face that clearly looked like a person that had not had much sleep. "And your shirt is on backwards," Jenny acknowledged, turning herself away from the TV program she was watching. "Come here…hold your arms up," Jenny instructed Lilliana. Lilliana raised her arms up while Jenny removed her pink t-shirt and turned it around, pulling it back down over her. "See, doesn't that feel better?" Jenny asked.

"I guess so," Lilliana replied.

Lilliana reminded Jenny so much of herself. Daniel was Spanish, as was his father, but his mother was born and raised in the United States, Colorado actually. Even Daniel, despite his fluent Spanish, would easily pass for an American. So it was no surprise that Lilliana resembled her in so many ways, even her blonde hair. That was a big shocker. Daniel always joked about that. About how despite his heritage and the fact that his mother was a brunette, that somehow, someway, Lilliana was blonde like her mother.

"Did you brush your teeth?" Jenny asked, walking to the kitchen area and opening the refrigerator to prepare for breakfast.

"I forgot," Lilliana said, as she began to click on the remote to her video game, making herself comfortable on the couch and knowing that she didn't have to go to school after all.

"No…no…no…young lady," Jenny said, closing the refrigerator and looking over at her. "Upstairs. Now!" Jenny ordered, as she laid the carton of eggs on the countertop.

Walking into the room revived from a fresh shower, Daniel offered Jenny a casual good morning kiss and headed straight for the coffee machine, his usual Sunday flip flops clicking against the tiled stone floor. His demeanor seemed a little off to Jenny. Normally he was quite a morning conversationalist, but today he went about his business in silence. Something was on his mind and she knew exactly what it was. As soon as he opened his mouth, it confirmed what she was thinking.

"It's not the first time you have talked in your sleep like that," he finally spoke, pulling out a chair and sitting down at the kitchen table with his cup of hot coffee in hand, blowing on it to cool it down.

"What?" Jenny asked, turning around after watching the two eggs she had just cracked sizzle against the heat of the pan.

"I guess you don't remember," Daniel surmised, taking a sip.

Actually, other than the nightmare she had had last night that was an accurate statement. As much as she tried, for the life of her, she couldn't remember any other previous dreams involving Dana.

"And?" she asked, questioning if he had any further information while holding the spatula in her hand.

"And what?" Daniel answered. "I don't know...like there's some girl named Dana." he paused, as he took another sip of his coffee before setting it down. "Apparently she's begging you to help her."

Agitated, Jenny turned back to the stove reluctantly to the sound of popping eggs. Flipping them, she wondered exactly how long these nightmares of hers had been going on. When she questioned him about that and he replied with a roundabout guess of two to three weeks, she could feel her blood beginning to boil and her face turning red with anger.

"You mean to tell me that my friend has been asking me to help her for weeks and you said nothing to me?!" she spat, slamming the spatula down and abandoning breakfast as she stormed over to him with her fists clenched. "Why didn't you tell me this before?" she demanded, placing her hands upon her hips.

He should have mentioned the nightmares she had been having, this he conceded to her. It was troublesome to him, but he struggled to understand her behavior.

"Why didn't you tell me this before, if you could hear me talking in my sleep?" she repeated.

"I mean...I don't know...is it really that important? I just thought..."

149

he began to explain, as he stepped by her to rescue their breakfast that was now beginning to smoke, permeating the room with a burnt smell.

"Yes! It is THAT important!" Jenny yelled, swiping her cigarette pack off the table and storming out of the house, allowing the screen door to slam shut behind her.

"Is mommy okay?" Lilliana asked, still sitting on the couch watching her cartoons and hearing the entire conversation.

"Mommy is just a little tired Lily," Daniel said, coming over to her and picking her up from the couch, holding her in his arms and kissing her nose.

"Why don't you go upstairs and brush your teeth like Mommy asked, and then we'll have breakfast," he suggested.

"Okay," she said, leaving to go upstairs.

"So, you need to talk to me," Daniel said, opening the screen door and seeing Jenny sitting on the front steps.

"I can't," Jenny said, as she took a drag from her cigarette. "It's nothing."

"Oh, it's nothing," Daniel repeated sarcastically. "I see. So, it's nothing that you're getting your daughter upset. It's nothing that you have kept me up half the night for weeks on end. It's nothing that you sound like a crazy person?"

"Don't say that to me," Jenny said back.

"Well, it's true," Daniel replied, standing over her.

"I mean, don't say that I'm crazy," Jenny said, beginning to cry.

Daniel could obviously tell she was distraught and it pained him to see her cry. "Hey," he said sitting down on the step beside her and putting his arm around her. "I didn't mean it that way, okay?" he said calmly, caressing her back through her nightgown.

"I'm not crazy," Jenny reiterated, still crying.

"I know. I know," Daniel assured her.

"God, there's just so much about me that you don't know, and I should have been more honest with you," she said, running her fingers through her hair with her head down.

"Okay, fair enough," Daniel replied. "Maybe when you feel like talking you can tell me some of these things," he said. "But in the meantime, I know enough. I know I love you with all of my heart. I know that I am lost without you. And I know we are blessed with a wonderful daughter."

"Thanks," Jenny said finally with a smile and kissing him.

"So, let's get some breakfast, right?" he asked, getting up.

"Right," she agreed, getting up as well.

...Later that night...

Jenny went to bed after what turned out to be a good day. In spite of the outburst she'd had with Daniel that morning, she actually felt good about herself and her life in general. Lilliana was tucked in bed, Daniel was sound asleep and snoring as usual. It would be a work day tomorrow, and she was fine with that. She liked the normalcy and daily routines in her world. It was something she'd never had before, but something she was beginning to get accustomed to. That was before she fell asleep...before the dreams began again.

"Jenny?" Dana asked. "Are you here?"

"Yes Dana, I am here," Jenny answered, but could not see her, only a black cloud.

"Take my hand," Dana said, reaching out from the darkness.

Jenny could see a hand protruding through what looked like black molasses. It was strange and almost had a liquid feel to it. Well, at least that's how she interpreted it to be.

"Why have you not answered me?" Dana asked, grabbing Jenny's hand to pull her through the dark mass.

"I...I wasn't sure Dana," Jenny replied, not really knowing the correct answer. "I thought maybe I was just losing my mind."

"You have not," Dana assured her, as her grip tightened and thrust

Jenny into a different realm.

"Here, I cannot help you," Dana instructed. "You must go on your way alone."

"Go where?" Jenny asked, looking at what appeared to be a dark lit tunnel, knee deep in water and infested with rats. She noticed factory type lighting fixtures placed every so often along the ceiling as far as she could see. The ones that were working provided dim but ample lighting, but many of them fluttered on and off in the darkness, creating an eerie and unsettling strobe light effect against the damp stone walls. It was as if she were back at Elizabeth's mansion, only worse...definitely worse. It reminded her of being in the subway tunnels in New York City at two in the morning, and there was no one around to look after you. "I must be crazy for doing this," she said to herself, trudging through the murky water in her nightgown and fighting off the rats swimming next to her. "Dana, are you here?" she asked.

"Follow the tunnel," her voice responded.

"To where?" Jenny asked, but there was no answer. "This is ridiculous," she thought after about 10 minutes had gone by, and she stopped to rest. "I need a cigarette," Jenny said, pulling a pack out from her nightgown shirt pocket and fumbling momentarily for her lighter before it was lit. Suddenly, before she could even exhale the smoke from her lungs, a figure appeared in the distance approaching her.

"You do not belong here," it spoke, as it drew nearer to her. She could tell from where she was standing that he was rather tall and wearing a long black leather trench coat that splashed through the water as he walked with a quick and angered stride. "Why are you here?" he asked upon meeting her face to face. His skin was like that of the moon, as pale white as one could imagine. He had no hair and his eyes were rolled back in his head, blind to anyone that would think differently.

"I know I don't belong here, but neither does my friend," Jenny answered, horrified at the sight of him, but standing her ground nonetheless. He paused for a moment...maybe 30 seconds... before answering.

"If you are referring to your friend Dana, I cannot help you and you must return to your world," he finally said.

"How do you know her?" she asked, bewildered and taking a drag off of her cigarette to keep her calm. "And how do you know me?"

"I know everything," he answered. "I am the gatekeeper."

"But aren't there four of you?" she asked, remembering the story Dana had told her.

"That is correct," he answered after another long pause.

"What is your name?" Jenny asked.

"My name?" he answered confused.

"Yeah, your name," Jenny answered. "You know...like what was your name before you became...well...you know...who you are."

"I...I don't remember my name," he answered, obviously becoming uneasy. "An eye for an eye, a soul for a soul," he shot back from his confusion. "That was the deal. That which has been done cannot be changed."

"Then I request counsel," Jenny demanded. "I wish my request to be judged."

"Very well," he answered, disappearing into thin air.

"Shit..." Jenny said to herself, pulling the last drag of her cigarette and tossing it into the water beneath her.

"You have requested to be judged," came a voice, as four gatekeepers appeared before her instantly. Honestly, they all looked the same with the exception that two of them appeared, by the wrinkles on their faces, to be elders.

"I do," Jenny confirmed.

"Who are you to come here and request such a thing?" spoke one of the elders.

"You are a mortal," said the second.

153

"Yes, I know, but my friend doesn't belong here," Jenny began. "She is a good person. She was tricked."

"You are referring to Elizabeth Franklin," the elder that Jenny took as being the one in charge spoke.

"Yes," Jenny simply answered.

"We would much rather have her soul," he stated. "But the deal was made by the Witches' Code. It cannot be broken."

"An eye for an eye. A soul for a soul," the first gatekeeper Jenny met repeated.

"But you were tricked!" Jenny exclaimed. "Just like my friend was. Are you really going to let her get away with this?"

"Perhaps the mortal is right," the second elder said. "It is her soul that we seek."

"Then release my friend!" Jenny exclaimed.

"Not so fast," came the first elder. "Your friend remains."

"Why? And for how long?" Jenny asked, raising her voice.

"Return to your world and do not come back here again," the first elder said with a pointed finger. "It is I that will decide my own council...not you!"

"But I can help," Jenny argued.

"You will leave here now or it is your soul I will take!" commanded the elder.

"Fine, then take my soul and release my friend...now!" Jenny screamed, extending her arms out in the air to define her point.

"Hmm...," the elder said, moving into Jenny's face, almost nose to nose. "You came here uninvited...you come here undead as a mortal... and you place demands upon...ME!!" he screamed, spitting in her face as he spoke through rotten teeth. "As a gatekeeper I am bound by certain rules, certain duties...but you are testing my patience child!"

"Let me see if I get this right," Jenny said, reaching for another cigarette and lighting it, much to the displeasure of the first elder.

"First Elizabeth escapes here, cheating you out of her soul. Then she cheats death, kills my friend, becomes a mortal…once again cheating you out of her soul…and all you have to show for it is the soul of an innocent girl that did nothing to deserve to be here. Sounds like you got a shitty deal."

"I am quite aware of that," the first elder replied, as he ripped the cigarette from her fingers and tossed it into the water beneath them. "Now let me make myself clear," he continued, again directly in her face. "You are in no position to come here and bargain with me. You are less than the putrid air of which I breathe. You asked to be judged and you have heard my council. Now, despite your arrogant behavior, I will consider your request."

"Thank you," Jenny replied, taking a step back to clear some distance between them.

"Do not indulge me with your courtesy," he said back. "Leave this place and do not return."

15

DANA'S CURSE

"Cracked skin and wrinkles gained,
I beseech my words to be shown upon thee,
Drown the youth from your face,
So that only your true age revealed shall be."

...*Elizabeth*...

"Good choice of wine," the man said from behind the counter, as Elizabeth set the bottle down. "Actually, it's the most expensive one we sell."

"I'm charmed," Elizabeth said, removing her sunglasses and reaching into her purse.

"That will be $47.50," he said, as he placed the bottle into a brown paper bag.

"You can keep the change," she said, handing him a fifty dollar bill.

"Do you have an ID ma'am?" the man asked.

"What is it with you people and your ID's?" she returned. "Do you have any idea how old I am?" she asked.

"Well, I'm guessing you're not 21, that's why I'm asking," he answered.

Elizabeth had been through this many times already. It was a blessing and a curse for having such a young face. In her time it wouldn't have mattered. There was no such thing as an ID then. Of course, she could have shown him. She was 23 and kept her ID current. It just wasn't her style. "Do I take your breath away?" she asked him, looking around to make sure no one was around.

"Well, I mean yes, you're very attractive but…" he began to answer before starting to choke.

"In about 10 seconds the air in your lungs will expire," Elizabeth said, with her now glowing blue eyes. "It would be a pity to kill you over what you presumptuously consider an expensive bottle of wine."

"Take it," he gasped, pushing the bottle to her.

"Well, I intended to anyway," she answered, dropping the fifty on the counter and walking away. "Oh...," she said, stopping at the door to put her sunglasses back on. "You may breathe now. Hahaha!" she laughed stepping outside. "Works every time."

"Robert," Elizabeth said into her phone moments later.

"Yes ma'am," he replied.

"You may draw my bath now," she said. "I will arrive home shortly."

"Yes ma'am," he acknowledged and waited for further instructions.

"That will be all," she said hanging up.

Elizabeth was rich beyond comparison. After cashing out the gold bars Jenny had found, she decided to leave the mansion for something more exquisite and updated. She bought the first penthouse suite she could find available in New York City. There it was easy to find a butler. One that would wait on you hand and foot as long as you paid them well. It wasn't quite the same as having a slave, but close. Her butler was in fact a black man, although his name wasn't Robert. It was Thomas. She just preferred to call him Robert. It was more fitting in such a way that even though Robert was dead, she could continue insulting him. The only things she kept from the mansion were her favorite gowns, the Witches' Bible, and Dana's GT Mustang. She loved driving it.

...30 minutes later...

"Robert," Elizabeth called out, laying in quite a large bathtub full of bubbles and resting her bare leg out of the water along the edge.

"Yes ma'am," Robert acknowledged, opening the bathroom door. He was dressed, as she was accustomed to seeing him, in a black suit and tie with a white shirt. With regard to attire, that at least hadn't changed from the world she knew.

"My glass seems to need refilling," she said, holding out her empty glass. Elizabeth watched his eyes as he approached her to take it. It was amusing to her, almost comical actually, how he tried to complete the task of pouring wine from a bottle and sneak a peek at her naked body. All the while making small talk about how her day was, as if that would distract her from noticing what was blatantly obvious. After such a boring day, she decided to have some fun with him at his expense.

"Robert, do you think I'm pretty?" she asked, as he handed her the filled glass and once again caught a glimpse of her bare leg.

"That's not my place to say ma'am," he answered, becoming uneasy.

"Do you want to fuck me?" she asked, taking a sip.

"Ma'am, please," Robert answered politely.

"Well, it's a simple question isn't it?" she asked. "Do you want to fuck me?"

"I'd rather not answer that ma'am," he replied.

"Really?" she asked. "Well, the way you were staring at my leg, I think you've already answered the question."

"I'm sorry ma'am. I meant no disrespect," he said.

"Hmm," she said, swirling the glass in her hand momentarily. "Then next time don't let your eyes speak for your tongue."

"Yes, ma'am," he said, staring down at his shoes.

"That will be all for now," she returned, watching his injured ego leave the room.

Elizabeth withdrew herself from the bathtub to dry off and proceeded to the mirror, wine glass in hand. As of yet, she still wasn't used to wearing makeup and felt the need to remove it. "That's rather peculiar," she thought to herself, noticing slight wrinkles under both of her eyes. "Peculiar indeed," she said out loud, pushing on them with her finger and leaning closer to the mirror. They weren't in any way considerable, but for a 23-year-old body they caught her attention. "Hmm," she thought, shrugging it off as she continued to wipe her face with a cotton swab in hand.

...Jenny...

Jenny awoke from her dream the following morning. Noticing the empty bed beside her, she glanced over to the clock and realized she had slept in. It was already 9 o'clock, exactly the time she was supposed to be at work.

"Shit," she said, climbing out of bed and rushing to her closet.

Daniel had left two hours ago, and Lilliana was already at school. They had agreed he would take her the previous night, so she was all alone with nobody to wake her up. And she hated alarm clocks. They were simply too annoying. Rummaging through the clothes hanging in the closet, sliding each dress one by one across the wooden pole with rejection, she suddenly paused...her hand still on the next clothes' hanger. She remembered the box she had stashed on the top shelf above her. Reaching for the chair by her makeup table, she set it in front of her and climbed up on it. Leaning over a pile of winter clothes, she found the box hidden behind them and pulled it out. "Maybe there's a way," she thought to herself, opening the box to reassure herself the game was still inside. At the last minute, before she closed the door forever to her room at the mental institution, she had grabbed the game and slid it into her dress pocket. Five years later, it had remained untouched. Halloween would be in 3 weeks. She would fly back with the game to Elizabeth's mansion and once again open the door. But she would have to tell Dana. Dana would have to be ready. "And then what?" Jenny thought. "This is crazy," she said to herself out loud, putting the game back. "I'm crazy," she added. "And late for work."

...Later that day...

"Hey Jenny, you got a minute?" Peter Stoltz asked with a New York accent, peeking into her small cubicle office, with a folder in his hand.

He was a middle aged man, unshaven for at least two days and sporting a sizeable gut in his midsection. It was hidden slightly by an oversized and wrinkled t-shirt that suggested he spent more time chasing down stories than worrying about his own personal appearance. His hair was the only thing resembling intentional maintenance, black and well groomed, parted down the middle and just above shoulder length.

"Sure, what's up?" she asked, spinning her chair around from her computer screen to face him. "Just downloading files...you know...the usual stuff."

"Well if you're bored, then you might like this," he said, stepping inside and handing her the file.

"What is it?" she asked, taking it from him.

"Copies of newspaper articles, magazine articles, photographs, tons of stuff," he answered. "Boss says he wants you to put a story together for Halloween."

Curiosity and excitement filled her face as she began to open the folder. She had always wanted to write for a magazine company or become a columnist for a newspaper. She had natural writing abilities as a teenager and was an editor for her high school paper. It was her intention to go to college and get her degree, had she not let gaming obscure her priorities. This was the chance she had been waiting for. Judging by Peter's smile, he knew how much it would mean to her. Opening the file, the smile on her face diminished instantly.

"I can't write about this!" she exclaimed, after seeing a picture of the

Franklin mansion and closing it.

"Why not?" Peter asked surprised. "Some really creepy things went on in that house. The owner, Mrs. Franklin, was a witch. Supposedly the daughter killed her and..."

"Yeah, I know!" Jenny interrupted him, suddenly feeling the urge for a cigarette.

"Oh," Peter said. "C'mon, it's a great piece to do for Halloween."

"Somebody already wrote a book about it," Jenny informed him bluntly.

"Oh," Peter replied, unaware of the book. "Yeah, but how long ago?" he rebounded, trying to sell her his pitch. "And they're tearing it down so..."

"What?! When?" Jenny exclaimed, asking and feeling a sickness in her stomach.

"I don't know, right after Halloween I think," he answered. "Well," he started to laugh, "apparently it's some local contracting company doing the demolition and they're afraid to go near it...I mean if you believe in all of that, right?...So anyway, they won't schedule the work until after Halloween. Jenny?" he asked, noticing a blank stare on her face. "Hello?" he said, snapping his finger. "Are you listening?"

"I need a cigarette," she said, standing up and handing the folder back to him.

"But...well wait a second," he stood holding the folder and bewildered, as Jenny walked past him with a lighter and a pack of cigarettes in her hand. "Did I say something wrong?" he yelled to her back as she was heading for the door.

Jenny leaned against the brick building and lit her cigarette with shaking hands, the busy sounds of traffic and honking horns not even registering to her ears. If that house is torn down, any chance of freeing Dana would be lost forever. The only way to open the door again is with her game...in that house...on Halloween night. That's it. There was no point in questioning why, she just knew it to be true. "Shit," she said taking a long drag and exhaling, tossing the remaining cigarette onto the street.

...moments later...

"Jenny, can I just talk to you for a minute?" Peter asked, following her back to her cubicle.

"I need to use the computer," she said, heading straight for her desk.

"Okay," Peter said, still confused and watching her. "Where are you flying to?" he asked a moment later, peering over her shoulder, practically breathing on her as he noticed an airline company pop up on her screen. "Beckon County?" he said with curiosity, as Jenny typed the words into the destination column.

"Do you mind?!" she crammed her neck back in his direction.

Peter took a step back to give her space, while he rummaged through the file in his hand. He was certain he had read that name somewhere. "Yeah, that's what I thought," he said, finding what he was looking for. "Beckon County...that's where the Franklin mansion is. So, you're going there?"

"You know, you sure ask a lot of questions," Jenny said, spinning around in her chair to face him annoyed.

"Of course, I'm a reporter," he said, shrugging his shoulders.

"Give me the folder," Jenny said with her hand out.

"So, you'll do the story?" he asked, handing it to her.

"Yes, now will you please get out of here!" she answered. "You're annoying me."

"Must have been one hell of a cigarette," he said under his breath, walking away.

"What?" Jenny asked.

"Nothing. Just nothing," he answered with his hands in the air.

Accepting the story would be the only way she could fly there and keep her job, and the only reason she could give Daniel for going there in the first place. It just is what it is. Then, of course, there was the mental institution issue. Would they still be looking for her after all this time? It was a chance she would have to take.

...That evening...

"Didn't you say you grew up in Beckon County?" Daniel asked Jenny, sifting through the articles and pictures from her folder spread out across the kitchen glass tabletop.

"Yep," Jenny agreed, casually picking up an article and pretending to be interested.

"And you never heard of this place?" he asked.

"Nope," she answered lying.

"Strange," he said, staring at a colored photograph.

"Why is it strange?" Jenny asked defensively.

"No, I mean this picture," he said, leaning over to show Jenny. "If you look in that window up there," he said pointing, "doesn't that look to you like a ghost with glowing blue eyes?"

"When was that picture taken?" Jenny asked, all too familiar with the blue eyes.

"I don't know, but there's a newspaper article attached to it," he said, flipping over the picture stapled to it. September 22, 2019," he noted from the article and began reading it to her. "Yesterday, an 18 year old man, Justin Clast, was found dead at an abandoned Civil War era plantation home in Beckon County. After being reported missing for several days, local authorities acted on an anonymous tip that had led them to the scene. Following an examination by the county coroner's office, it was determined based on the location of his body that he had fallen down a flight of stairs in the house and suffered multiple fractures and a broken neck. No foul play has been considered and the incident has been ruled accidental. However, this picture taken later that evening by a local reporter, may prove otherwise. Many residents here believe the house, referred to as the Franklin Mansion, is haunted and that the young man's death was at the hands of the deceased original owner, Mary Franklin."

"That's impossible," Jenny stated.

"What, the picture?" Daniel asked. "Well true, anyone could photo-edit a ghost in a window."

"No, I mean Mary Franklin," Jenny corrected him. "She wasn't there. This photograph of a ghost with blue eyes was taken four days later."

"Yeah, so?" Daniel asked.

"So, Elizabeth couldn't have been a ghost. And it definitely wasn't her mother." she concluded.

"Who's Elizabeth?" he asked confused. "And I thought you said you had never heard of the Franklin Mansion before."

"Oh…well…" Jenny began to backtrack, after getting lost in the conversation. "No, of course not. But I've been doing some research."

"Alright, so how do you explain the picture then?" he asked.

"Like you said…probably photo-edited," she answered, but knowing there was much more to it than that.

…Elizabeth…

Elizabeth awoke the following morning, despite a peaceful and uninterrupted sleep, feeling exhausted. Climbing out of bed, she immediately felt nauseous as her feet hit the floor, walking slowly with one hand on her stomach as she reached the bathroom mirror and flipped the light on.

"Noooo!" she cried out reaching for her face. The wrinkles under her eyes that she had noticed just last night were even worse than before, and small wrinkles were beginning to form around the edges of her mouth.

"Ma'am?" came the voice from behind her bedroom door, followed by a knock.

"What is it Robert?" Elizabeth answered the way one would when you didn't want to be disturbed.

"I have your breakfast and tea ma'am," he replied.

"Very well, come in," she said reluctantly, while she pulled her nightgown tighter across her chest.

"I'll just set it over here since you're already up," he said, noticing her standing near the bathroom door and carefully placing the tray on a small glass table top. "Are you okay?" he asked, looking closer at her as she stood silent watching him and leaning against the door frame. "Ma'am?" he asked with concern, walking closer to her. "Are you feeling okay? You don't look so good."

"Correct me if I'm wrong, but I don't recall hearing my voice asking your opinion on how I look" Elizabeth answered angrily.

"I'm just concerned, that's all," Robert replied.

"Concern yourself with other matters," she said coldly.

"Yes ma'am," he said standing still.

"You may leave," she added.

Robert left the room, closing the door behind him. Elizabeth tried to eat, but her stomach would not allow it. Only the tea seemed soothing. Standing there beside the small glass coffee table, she stared down into the cup she was holding, slowly swirling her spoon in the tea and realized what she needed to do.

Later that night, Elizabeth closed the door to a room filled with candles located at the far end of her penthouse suite. She was wearing a black dress-like cape and hood and carried the Witches' Bible in her right hand. Only the glow of her blue eyes and the flickering of flames lit the otherwise dark room. Standing next to a large cauldron set on a 3 legged iron stand, Elizabeth recited two separate carefully chosen verses from the book and placed it on a table next to her. Watching as the water inside the cauldron began to shimmer, she moved closer to it and waited.

"I've been expecting you to call upon me," her grandmother's face spoke from the rippling water, somewhat distorting her appearance.

"Why is this body rejecting me?" Elizabeth asked, looking down into the water.

"She is fighting you," her grandmother answered.

"She's not a witch," Elizabeth stated.

"She has cursed you nonetheless," her grandmother replied. "She has turned the pain and suffering her soul has endured into hatred," she continued. "It is from this hatred fueled by her presence in hell that her power derives. She is quite dangerous."

"What will happen to me?" Elizabeth asked.

"Even for me it is difficult to predict the future," her grandmother answered.

"Will I die?" Elizabeth stated.

"Unless the curse is broken…yes," she answered.

"Will a sacrifice break the curse?" Elizabeth asked.

"Perhaps, yes," her grandmother agreed. "The stronger her powers, the stronger the curse."

Elizabeth stood silent, as the anger inside her swelled. She could feel the energy radiate from her eyes as her face tuned to a skeleton.

"I will not die at the hands of a mortal!" she screamed, pointing to her grandmother's reflection with an outreached finger.

"I understand child," her grandmother answered. "Do what you must do." And with that said, her face disappeared, leaving only the reflection of Elizabeth's skull and raging blue eyes looking down into the water.

…An hour later…

"Nah bro, I don't care how she talks to me," Robert said, sitting in the kitchen with his cell phone in one hand and a glass of wine in the other. "That crazy white bitch pays me over a hundred thousand a year dog…in cash! What?" Robert asked his friend on the other end of the phone call. "Shit man…I mean I don't know…" Robert began to answer his friend's question. "I mean I could've fucked her last night but who knows, and I ain't about to throw this kinda money away for a piece of ass…know what I'm sayin?"

"Robert?" he could hear Elizabeth calling from the other room.

"Shit, I gotta go," he said quickly and hung up on his friend.

"Why are you in the kitchen so late?" Elizabeth asked, walking in.

"Just…ah…just having a glass of wine ma'am," he answered.

"Hmm," she said, looking around the kitchen and then back to him.

"Well if wine is your preference for the evening, I think you will find the bottle I'm drinking much more to your satisfaction," she suggested.

"Ma'am?" he questioned.

"Oh for God's sake!" Elizabeth said annoyed. "Must you always be so ignorant to my requests?"

"No ma'am," Robert said, setting his glass down and standing up smiling.

"Right this way," she said, leaving the kitchen to the adjacent room, equipped with a full bar and all of the amenities an entertainment center could provide. "Sit down." Elizabeth ordered, reaching for an empty glass at the service bar, as Robert followed her in and took his place on her couch as instructed. "Would you like a cube of ice?" she asked, preparing the drink with her back turned to him, showing her ass from the see-through black nightgown she was wearing.

"That would be great ma'am," Robert answered, sitting there in complete bewilderment but becoming aroused.

"Must you sit there in your black tie and suit the entire evening, or are you too naïve to understand what's going on?" Elizabeth asked, turning to him with a wine glass in her hand.

"No ma'am!" Robert answered, as he immediately began to remove his clothes.

"At least for tonight…" Elizabeth said, turning back around to the service bar and emptying the contents of a small vial of poison into his glass…"you will refer to me as Elizabeth."

"Yes, ma'am," he said. "I…I mean Elizabeth."

"That's much better," she said, approaching him in a provocative manner and handing him the glass of wine.

"Now drink up," she said, raising her own glass of wine. "We have much better things to do."

"Damn right," he agreed, taking the glass from her and taking it down in one long swallow.

"Hmm," she noted from how quick he consumed his drink. "That was much easier than I thought it would be."

"Damn, what kind of wine is this?" he asked, becoming delirious and trying to set his empty glass down, missing the table in front of him entirely as it crashed onto the marble floor beneath him.

"The kind that renders you useless," Elizabeth answered with a smile, taking a sip from her own wine glass and observing his shirtless limp body on the couch in front of her. "It's a pity actually," she said staring at him. "I might have enjoyed it."

Elizabeth drug his unconscious body to the room she had spoken to her grandmother from and heaved his body onto the long wooden table, strapping his arms and legs down with restraints. Satisfied he was secured tightly, she opened the Witches' Bible to the necessary page and opened an ornately decorated black box, revealing her grandmother's sacrificial knife. She was ready.

"Where am I?" Robert came to and asked, slightly slurring his words. The poison she had used on him was in fact quite strong, but it doesn't last long. That was its only drawback. In this case, however, the timing couldn't have been any better.

"What happened to me?" he asked, now noticing his chain restraints and testing them with resistance. "What the fuck?!" he yelled, yanking hard against them to no avail.

"Shhh," Elizabeth said, standing over him in her black negligee. "This will be over soon."

"See man, I knew you were crazy!" he yelled, continuing to fight against the chains, creating a loud clanging sound against the wooden surface. "Shit," he said, looking around the room at the dozens of lit candles as he began to perspire. "You're a witch, aren't you?" he asked, looking up at her as her eyes began to glow immensely.

"That is correct," she answered, suddenly thrusting her hand to his throat and squeezing it tightly. "And if you don't shut up, I'm going to rip your tongue out and make you eat it!" she warned him.

Robert could feel her overwhelming strength and lay motionless and quiet until he was relieved off her grip. "Please ma'am, I don't want to die," he begged.

Ignoring his plea, Elizabeth reached for the Witches' Bible and began to recite. "Release the curse that has stricken me, by the Witches' Code I implore. In return I offer this soul to thee, so that the curse can be no more."

"Let me go…please!" he begged.

"This is going to hurt," she simply stated, as she reached for the knife and immediately plunged it into his heart, spewing blood across her face and her partially exposed breasts.

"Ahhhh!" he screamed in agony, his body involuntarily sitting up as far as the chains would allow and then slamming back down onto the table. Elizabeth held onto the knife as blue sparks and electricity began to envelope his body. Robert's eyes rolled back in his head, as the last breath of air escaped his open mouth. His lifeless body jumped and spasmed against the chains. In a sudden flash, a burst of blue energy shot through the knife and into Elizabeth, rendering her unconscious and she fell helplessly to the floor.

Waking up only moments later, Elizabeth grabbed the knife lying next to her hand and pulled herself up from the floor. Noticing that only a pile of ash remained of Robert, she realized it was over. But did it work? That was the question that begged to be answered. Elizabeth closed the Witches' Bible and returned her grandmother's knife to the box before heading to the nearest bathroom mirror. She didn't want to be overconfident. But she could feel her usual vibrant self again, and the pain in her stomach had vanished. "Mirror, mirror on the wall," she laughed in jest, as she switched on the bathroom light to look, discovering her face and gown were covered in blood. Elizabeth stripped from her negligee and stood naked in front of the mirror as she wiped the blood from her face and breasts, occasionally rinsing the washcloth.

"Hahaha!" she finally rejoiced with a smile and laughing. It had worked. Her skin was perfect. In fact, she looked even younger than she had before the curse had started its aging process. Leaving the bathroom and her bloodstained negligee, Elizabeth walked to the bar and poured herself a glass of wine. "Thank you my dear Robert," she said, holding up her glass to his clothes laying haphazardly on the couch. "Thank you, indeed."

16

SISTERHOOD

"The future is said to be untold,
but for you, your path, by your own accord,
has been predetermined.
Have faith in it and you shall prevail."

…Jenny…a week later…

"Come tell mommy goodbye Lily honey," Jenny said, seeing the cab arrive from the kitchen window. Lilliana set down her glass of orange juice and crawled out from under the covers that comforted her while she watched cartoons.

"I don't want you to go," she whined, getting off the couch to head for the adjacent kitchen.

"I know," Jenny said, leaning down with open arms to embrace her. "But I won't be gone long, maybe just a week," she said, hugging her tightly.

"Promise?" Lilliana asked, hugging her mom back.

"Promise," Jenny said, kissing her cheek. "You be a good girl, okay?"

"I'm always a good girl," Lilliana said.

"Yes you are," Jenny said, standing up as Lilliana wrapped her arms around her leg.

"Looks like somebody doesn't want you to go," Daniel said, coming into the room with Jenny's suitcase.

"Breaks my heart," Jenny replied, playing with Lilliana's hair.

"Lily, can Daddy talk to mommy alone for a minute?" he said to her.

"Alright," she answered with a sad voice and left to return to her cartoons.

"Look, I know that there's more to this than you're telling me, so please be careful, okay?" he asked, reaching to take her hand.

"Oh c'mon," she attempted to laugh. "It's just a crazy old house and a few farmers with overactive imaginations."

"It's more than that and you know it," he said, looking into her eyes. "And I know it."

Jenny could feel a tear forming. She tried to withhold it, but it was no use as it began to roll down her cheek.

"Hold me," she said.

Daniel held her in his arms, not wanting to let go.

"I'll be careful," she said sniffling. "Seriously, I'll be fine," she assured him a moment later, pulling herself together and letting go of his embrace.

"Come on Lily, sweetheart, let's walk mommy to the car," he said to his little girl, reaching down to pick up the suitcase. Lilliana jumped up and followed Daniel and her mother out the front door to the cab awaiting.

"Oh, I forgot to tell you," Daniel began.

"I'll take that sir," the cab driver said, exiting the car and reaching for the suitcase.

"Somebody called for you while you were in the shower," he continued, handing over the suitcase and saying thank you.

"Who was it?" Jenny asked.

"He said his name was Robert," he answered. "Sounded like he works for your company."

"Robert?" Jenny asked, as a chill ran down her spine.

"Yeah, do you know him?" he asked.

"Um..sure...of course," she began to stutter, caught completely off guard. "He's uh...he's one of our editors," she lied as best she could, brushing the hair aside from her face in a nervous manner. "What did he say?"

"He said there's something you need to know about your friend Dana, the one you have dreams about," Daniel answered. "I guess it's for the story you're going to write."

"That's it? That's all he said?" Jenny asked, wanting to know more.

"He just said he would explain later," Daniel answered.

"I see," Jenny said with a blank expression, as if her mind was somewhere else.

"Are you okay?" Daniel asked, noticing a concerned look on her face. "What's this all about?" he questioned.

"I don't know," she answered. "I really don't know."

...Elizabeth...

The following day Elizabeth awoke from a relaxing sleep to the morning sunrise edging its way ever so slowly across the darkened room until finally reaching her bed and casting a warm glow upon her youthful face. Stretching her arms from beneath the comfort of her white satin sheets, she yawned briefly and sat up. Looking around her room, it dawned on her that there would be no breakfast awaiting her. Only the loneliness of a large penthouse suite.

"Pity," she said to herself, climbing out of the bed and reaching for her phone.

"Good morning Miss Franklin," a voice came from her phone only a moment later, recognizing her name and aware she was the owner of the most expensive penthouse suite in the building.

"That is of yet to be determined," she replied. "It seems as though my butler has taken a leave of absence from me."

"I'm sorry to hear that ma'am," he returned. "Is there something I can do for you?"

"Would you be a dear and send some tea?" she requested.

"Of course Miss Franklin, tea and breakfast. Our pleasure," he obliged.

Moments later, Elizabeth was sipping her tea and sitting with her laptop at her kitchen table. There was something she had been wanting to do.

"Let's see what I can find out about you bitch," Elizabeth said, as her fingers typed the words...Dana Reynolds...onto the keyboard. "Hmm," she thought, staring at the screen that brought up hundreds of matches for that name. "Narrow search," she read from the list of options and clicked on it. "State...South Carolina," she typed in. "County...Beckon," she continued typing.

We found 5 results for Dana Reynolds that match your search criteria:

Dana Reynolds, 45, Beckon County, SC

Dana Reynolds, 32, Beckon County, SC

Dana Reynolds, 60, Beckon County, SC

Dana Reynolds, 51, Beckon County, SC

Dana Reynolds, 23, Beckon County, SC

Elizabeth clicked on the last entry and waited. "And there you are," she said, as the computer screen paused momentarily before bringing up a picture of Dana with a brief biography below it.

Dana Reynolds: current age 23

Date of Birth: 11/23/1994

Place of Birth: Beckon County

Current residence: New York

Adopted (click here for public records)

"Adopted," Elizabeth read surprised and clicked the link.

Adopted – 1/12/1995

Adoptive parents: Frank and Laura Reynolds

Birth parents: Nathan and Sheila Franklin

"Franklin!!" Elizabeth exclaimed, leaning into the screen in disbelief. "It can't be," she said, reaching for her tea to take a sip and then continuing on.

Elizabeth spent the next hour researching the genealogy of Nathan Franklin, making certain she had the correct person behind the name until finally the results stared at her from her laptop.

Nathan Franklin – 1977, Patrick Franklin – 1955, Henry Franklin – 1934, Winfield Franklin – 1911, John Franklin – 1890, George Franklin – 1867, Winfield Franklin – 1848, John Franklin – 1829, Lawrence Franklin – 1828.

"Oh dear God!" Elizabeth gasped with her hand over her mouth seeing her father's name Lawrence. "What have I done?!" she cried out, as her hands began to shake. "She's a Franklin...she has witches' blood!"

...later that evening...

"Why didn't you tell me!?" Elizabeth asked angrily to the reflection of her grandmother's face rippling in the cauldron's water.

"To what extent would the truth have mattered?" she answered her. "Like your mother, she is gone."

"I am ashamed of what I have become," Elizabeth said solemnly, hanging her black cloaked head down. "I have once again violated the Witches' Code."

"What you have become is a most powerful witch," her grandmother spoke. "You possess the powers thrice fold of yours, your mothers... and now Dana Franklins."

"I have become a freak and a murderer!" Elizabeth yelled, throwing the wine glass she was holding and shattering it against the white wall, leaving red wine trailing down it like blood.

"I will not hear of that child!" her grandmother yelled. "It is I that taught you to embrace your power when your mother would have nothing of it. I nurtured you while she held you back. Unfortunate, yes…but necessary that she had to die."

"How can you say that?" Elizabeth asked, as the anger inside her grew, intensifying the glow in her eyes. She tried to control it, but it was impossible.

"Should you not have destroyed Dana Franklin, you would have been sent back to hell," her grandmother pushed on.

Her heart was pounding in her chest. The betrayal of her own thoughts fought her emotions as her grandmother's voice reverberated in her head.

"You would not be standing before me in her body," she went on, until finally…

"Perhaps it is you that should be destroyed!" Elizabeth spoke from her skeleton face.

"Much better child," her grandmother smiled with content. "And only from your hatred would you stand a chance."

"Careful grandmother," Elizabeth warned with a pointed finger and fiery blue eyes. "My allegiance to you is not unwavering."

"Then do not call upon me again," she said, as the smile left her face.

"I do not intend to!" Elizabeth yelled into the air, pushing the cauldron over with one hand and sending it flying effortlessly several feet into the air before landing on the floor. Elizabeth stood there in her black cape and hood breathing heavily and realizing her grandmother had created the monster inside her.

"Nooo!" she screamed from her skeleton teeth, looking up to the ceiling with fists clenched and expending every ounce of breath she had.

17

MARY FRANKLIN

"A revelation is brought to thee,
The truth is not what it is perceived to be."

...Jenny...

Jenny stood at the airport arrival gate texting Daniel as her cab pulled up. She had decided to go straight to the mansion, foregoing her hotel for now. There was plenty of time to check in, and she really wanted to have a look around. For whatever reason she didn't know, but Robert's message about Dana had her perplexed.

"There's something about Dana you need to know," were the words that played over and over in her head. "But what?" she kept asking herself. "What is it that I need to know?"

"How was your flight ma'am?" the cab driver asked, picking up her luggage and proceeding to the trunk of the car.

"Oh you know, the usual," Jenny replied. "Crowded, stuffy, uncomfortable and boring."

"Yeah, I know what you mean," he said, closing the trunk and opening the door for her. "Well, at least we have nice weather."

"It's surprising actually for this time of year," Jenny said, waiting to reply until the cab driver climbed in.

"Oh, so you're from around here," he noted buckling up and setting the meter.

"Born and raised," Jenny answered.

"So where to?" he asked.

"Well I don't have a house address, but it's on Crabtree Road," she answered. "Off Route 19."

"Crabtree Road," he repeated, punching the name in his navigator. "Oh, okay," he said as the map came up. "That's where the Franklin mansion is."

"That's where I'm going," she noted.

"Let me guess…reporter?" he asked, putting the car into motion.

"Writer," she answered. "I'm doing a story for Stargate magazine."

"Oh, wow," he said, impressed. "Yeah, I didn't even know about the mansion until they mentioned they were tearing it down on the news," he said, checking his mirror to change lanes. "You should talk to some of the locals. From what I hear a lot of them are direct descendants of the Franklin family."

"Really?" Jenny asked.

"Well, I don't know much about it," he confessed. "But the guy that built that place…Lawrence Franklin I think his name was…was some kind of business tycoon. He practically built this town."

"Interesting to know," Jenny admitted.

…One hour later…

"It looks even bigger in person," the cab driver noted, seeing the mansion towering into the sky from a distance.

"Home sweet home," Jenny said sarcastically.

"I'm not trying to scare you or anything," the driver said, continuing down the gravel road as they neared closer. "But from what I hear this place is supposedly haunted."

"Well aware," Jenny answered. "I mean that's pretty much why I'm writing the story."

"Do you want me to wait for you?" he asked. "I mean I can't just leave you out here in the middle of nowhere."

"I really don't know how long I will be," Jenny returned.

"Alright, well look," he said, reaching for his card and handing it back to her from over his seat. "When you're ready just call me. That's my direct number."

"Thank you," she said, taking the card.

"Well, here we are," the driver said moments later as he stopped the car as close to the house as he could get. "There's not much of a driveway there, so I hope this is okay," he apologized, noticing the overgrown weeds.

"No this is fine," Jenny said, reaching for her purse.

"Sixty even," he said, looking over at the meter.

"Keep the change," Jenny offered and handed him the money.

"Well, thank you," he said, taking it and opening his door. "I'll get your luggage. Say do you mind taking my picture?" he asked, reaching for his phone.

"Not at all," Jenny replied, climbing out and walking over to him.

"Just hit that button right there," he said, demonstrating and handing it over to her.

The cab driver took his place, with the mansion behind him in the background, as Jenny took the picture.

"How did it turn out?" he asked, walking to the trunk to retrieve her luggage.

"Let me see," she answered, zooming in on the picture with her fingers and noticing a pair of blue eyes looking out from the second story window.

"It's waiting for me," she said under her breath.

"What's that?" he asked, closing the trunk.

"Oh...ah nothing. It turned out good," she said, handing his phone back to him as he approached.

"Thanks," he said, setting the suitcase down next to her.

"Well, you be careful in there," he said, feeling bad leaving her all alone. "You never know about these old houses."

"I will, thanks," she said, grabbing the handle of her suitcase.

"And call me when you're ready," he said, climbing into the cab.

Jenny watched as the car drove away, coming to the realization that she was alone…but not entirely. Navigating her suitcase through the weeds would prove impossible, and she didn't really need it anyway, only her flashlight. Retrieving it, she hid the suitcase as best she could in the thick stalks and proceeded to the mansion.

"Hello?" she yelled out with an echo once inside. "I know you're in here," she yelled out again against the sounds of creaking boards beneath her feet. "Wow, this place is in worse shape than I thought it would be," she observed, as a small bird took off across the room in front of her and headed for a window that was missing most of its glass. The floor was covered in dried up grass and thistle most likely brought in from the wind, and pieces of white plaster that had fallen from the ceiling above. It had only been 5 years since she was last here, but time and neglect had finally started taking its toll. "No wonder they're tearing it down" she thought to herself walking towards the foyer. "Now see, that's just wrong," she noted, seeing a collection of empty beer cans laying discarded on the floor. "At least we cleaned up after ourselves."

"Hello?" she said once again, reaching the foyer and shining her flashlight up to the grand staircase. She could hear the crickets relentless chirping in the background, and she wasn't sure if that made her feel more comfortable or more alone. There were no windows here to allow moonlight in, with the exception of a pair that were covered with thick curtains. She had never felt more vulnerable in her life.

"Don't be afraid," came a voice, just as Jenny had directed her flashlight to the kitchen ahead.

"Robert?" she asked, stopping in her tracks and recognizing his voice.

"Yes," he answered.

Jenny turned around and shined her flashlight back up to the staircase.

"I would like you to make someone's acquaintance," his ghost form said, as her flashlight caught him staring down at her.

"Okay," Jenny said, clearing her throat and not knowing what to expect.

"Allow me to introduce to you Madam Franklin," he said.

"How do you do?" she asked, making her presence known from thin air next to Robert.

"Mary Franklin??" Jenny asked in disbelief.

"The same," she replied, beginning to descend down the stairs.

"This is too weird," Jenny thought to herself, watching Mary and Robert approach her. Robert was wearing black pants with a white shirt garnished with a black neck tie, and Mary was wearing what appeared to be an exquisite evening gown. Although the color was hard to make out as they were both, for the most part, transparent. Instinctively, she reached out to shake their hands, withdrawing her own almost immediately as she realized physical contact was impossible.

"In my time we were accustomed to a curtsy," Mary smiled, as she bowed with her knees, holding her dress up with both hands.

Jenny mimicked the curtsy in return, feeling absolutely ridiculous.

"May I ask your last name?" Mary asked.

"Aldren," Jenny provided.

"There is no need to be concerned Miss Aldren," Mary assured her, sensing Jenny's uneasiness. "I only wish to speak to you."

"Oh, please, call me Jenny," she insisted.

"It would not be proper," Mary replied.

There was no point in debating that. A lot of things in Jenny's world would have been considered improper to a time period where manners and respect came first and foremost.

"You messaged me about Dana," Jenny said, looking at Robert.

"Yes," he confirmed.

"Your friend, I presume?" Mary asked.

"A dear friend, yes," Jenny answered, wondering what this was about.

"She is a Franklin," Mary informed her.

"What?" Jenny reeled back in disbelief and doubting what she had just heard.

"She is a direct descendant of generations of witches," Mary informed her. "She is a direct descendant of myself and my husband."

"Wait…what?" Jenny asked again, shocked beyond belief. "It's impossible, she would have told me!"

"Had she have known, I am certain she would have," Mary agreed. "I am in great need of your help. Elizabeth and Dana are the last remaining bloodline of the Franklins. When you last created the gateway, the path between your world and ours, I tried to intervene. I tried to stop Elizabeth from violating the Witches' Code and destroying one of our sisters….your friend Dana. But I was too late, and the gateway closed. I am trapped here along with Robert, who was trying to help me."

"So you want me to open the gateway again?" Jenny asked, already knowing the answer.

"Yes, if you can," Mary said.

"I can, but then what?" Jenny asked.

"I will call upon Dana," Mary answered. "She will see the light, and she will come."

"I've tried to talk to her. I've tried to help her," Jenny assured. "She comes to me in my dreams."

"It is difficult for the living," Mary noted. "And hell has its grip on her soul."

"Yes," Jenny agreed.

"She can only escape if there is a clear path…on Hallows Eve," Mary stated. "As did my daughter."

"And Elizabeth?" Jenny asked.

"Unfortunately, without her my attempt to restore Dana to the living would be in vain," she answered.

Elizabeth would never agree to it as far as Jenny was concerned, and she relayed her doubts to Mary.

"My mother has tried to make her something she was not meant to be," Mary said. "I feel her anger and her sorrow. She will come."

"Yeah well, Dana felt her sorrow too and look where that got her," Jenny rebutted.

"I cannot expect you to understand Miss Aldren," Mary said. "But there is an undeniable bond between witches, between sisters. Had Elizabeth's judgement not been clouded by the evil my mother instilled upon her, she would never have done what she did…to Dana or to me."

"I hope you're right, because I don't trust her," Jenny said with conviction.

"I only request your trust in me," Mary replied.

"The last time I did this my friends all died," Jenny informed her. "It's hard for me to explain to you, but it's a game. It's a game that opens the gateway. One that I am not interested in ever playing again."

"It is out of the realm of my understanding," Mary admitted. "Elizabeth will know what to do. There is no need to worry, I assure you."

Assurance was a word that sometimes fell flat of its promise, but Jenny relented, parting ways with Mary and Robert and agreeing to call Elizabeth when she arrived at her hotel. She just hoped Elizabeth was still using Dana's phone.

18

PLOTS OF DECEIT

"Deception hides amongst shards of glass,
willing you to bleed before seeing it."

...Elizabeth...

It had been a day since the argument with her grandmother, and although time usually heals all wounds, in her case it had only made her more miserable. Even the empty bottle of wine, laying carelessly on her bedroom floor, did little to wash away her sins. Elizabeth lay on her bed staring out at the nighttime sky and the bright lit landscape of New York City crying uncontrollably. Even the feeling of being alive again had lost its luster and she couldn't even look at herself in the mirror without the reflection of Dana's face looking back at her. The guilt was literally eating her up inside. She didn't blame Dana for putting the curse on her. She deserved it, and quite honestly she would have done the same.

"Why didn't you tell me?" Elizabeth asked the empty room. "Why didn't you tell me grandmother?" she repeated. But she knew why. Her grandmother wanted her to take her place, to carry on the evil side of the Franklins. Only now did she realize why her mother would not use her powers to save her grandmother from death.

"You are behaving like a young adolescent fool," her grandmother's face spoke from the dresser mirror across the room from her bed.

"Leave me alone," Elizabeth said, rolling over and covering her head with a pillow.

"Dana will sense your sudden newfound sympathy for her and use your weakness to destroy you," her grandmother continued.

"Her curses are useless against me," Elizabeth stated from under her pillow. "And she will never escape from hell."

"That is where you are gravely mistaken," her grandmother said. "Your mother has spoken to an acquaintance of yours, Jenny Aldren."

"What?!" Elizabeth exclaimed, immediately removing the pillow and sitting up to address her. "How?" she asked, as anger began to replace her feelings of sorrow.

"Your mother tried to stop you from switching bodies with Dana," her grandmother began to explain. "She came through along with her putrid slave Robert, but it was too late."

"She's trapped," Elizabeth concluded.

"Indeed," her grandmother agreed. "But not for long."

"Jenny will open the door again," Elizabeth quickly reasoned.

"And Dana will be free from hell," her grandmother added. "Free to seek her vengeance upon you."

"I presume because of her curse upon me, she is aware of her heritage," Elizabeth surmised.

"Quite aware," her grandmother answered. "In death, all is revealed."

"I should have killed that bitch a long time ago," Elizabeth said referring to Jenny.

"She is the least of your problems," her grandmother stated.

"But Dana will be trapped, just as I was," Elizabeth said, realizing. "There is little she can do to me if she cannot walk amongst the living."

"I do not wish to talk with you in riddles my dear Elizabeth, so let me be frank," her grandmother began. "Your mother has made contact with our High Priestess. She will demand your presence and you cannot abstain from her request. She will reverse what you have done."

"And what happens to me?" Elizabeth asked, now becoming very concerned.

"You will be given leniency as you and Dana are the last remaining bloodlines," she answered.

"I will remain in this world?" Elizabeth asked.

"There will be a price to pay, but yes," her grandmother answered.

"What price?" Elizabeth asked.

"That I do not know," she answered. "There can only be one true heir to our bloodline, Elizabeth. Dana has Franklin blood, but it is not pure. It is tainted by generations of wretched men."

"I understand," Elizabeth agreed, succumbing once again to her grandmother's influence over her.

"So once the process is reversed, you will destroy the High Priestess, Dana, and your adversary Jenny Aldren," her grandmother ordered.

"Have you lost your mind Grandmother?!" Elizabeth exclaimed in shock at the suggestion to destroy the High Priestess. "Her powers are unmatched to mine. And besides, even to mutter such an idea from one's mouth would be an unthinkable violation to the Witches' Code."

"She will not expect it," her grandmother said. "This will be the first time in 500 years that she will be vulnerable in the land between the living and the dead."

"And if I fail?" Elizabeth asked.

"You will stab her from behind with the dagger I gave you," she answered. "From behind and through the heart."

"Hmm," Elizabeth pondered, now forgetting her sorrow and misery and becoming her old self again. "The powers I could possess would be…"

"You would have the power to bring even me back to walk amongst the living," he grandmother interrupted.

"Yes," Elizabeth agreed, getting up from her bed and walking over to stand in front of the mirror.

"And what of the Witches' Code?" she asked to her grandmother's smiling face.

"My dear child, you will be the new High Priestess," she answered. "There is no one with more authority to pass judgement upon you. Not even hell itself."

"I will be immortal!" Elizabeth exclaimed, smiling to herself.

"Yes!" her grandmother returned. "You will live for eternity."

...Jenny...

"So this should be interesting," Jenny said to herself, settling into her hotel room and reaching for her cell phone. "I'll be surprised if she even answers."

"Jenny Aldren I presume," a voice spoke from her phone a moment later. "I would say what a pleasant surprise, but then I would be speaking through a forked tongue wouldn't I?"

"Charming as usual," Jenny replied.

"Indeed," Elizabeth said. "And how is my mother?"

That caught Jenny completely off guard. She was not expecting her to know anything about the meeting she'd had with Mary Franklin. Not that it mattered to any degree of importance but unsettling nonetheless.

"Look, I'm just the messenger," Jenny stated, reaching in her purse for her cigarettes and lighter. "I didn't even know she would be there."

"Yes, but you came to my house just the same," Elizabeth replied. "May I ask why?"

"I don't know really," she answered, holding her phone between her shoulder and chin while lighting her cigarette.

"You would not have left had I been there," Elizabeth informed her. "I am growing tired of you and your friends presuming it is yours to do with as you please."

"I'm sorry," Jenny said, exhaling a puff of smoke and becoming slightly rattled. "You're right…I mean, it was wrong for me to go there."

"Well in this case, I will accept your apology," Elizabeth said. "So my mother wishes to see me?"

"How do you know all of this?" Jenny asked, perplexed.

"I am a witch or have you forgotten?" Elizabeth answered.

"No, of course not," Jenny replied.

"I was unaware Dana was our sister," Elizabeth stated. "Had I known, perhaps I would have chosen you."

"Haha!" Jenny laughed. "You wouldn't have tricked me so easily. I don't have sympathy for you like she did."

"You underestimate my powers Jenny Aldren," Elizabeth said.

"Maybe," Jenny admitted.

"No, most assuredly," she shot back.

"Well, since you seem to know so much about this, will you come or not?" Jenny asked point blank.

"How could I miss such a wonderful reunion?" Elizabeth asked sarcastically.

"And you will not harm me?" Jenny asked, knowing she couldn't trust her regardless of the answer.

"As tempting as that would be, it is not the purpose for this occasion," Elizabeth replied. "Your answer is no."

"I'm only doing this for Dana," Jenny said. "I could care less about you, you know that."

"Point well taken," Elizabeth said.

"See you on Halloween night then," Jenny concluded.

"Hallows Eve," Elizabeth corrected her.

"Damn, I keep getting that wrong," Jenny stated, snapping her finger.

"Until then," Elizabeth said, hanging up.

This was becoming way more than Jenny had bargained for. There was absolutely no way she could trust Elizabeth despite her assurances.

She would kill her without an ounce of hesitation if the chance arose. And why would Elizabeth agree so easily to reverse the spell on Dana? Something was wrong. A piece of the puzzle was definitely missing. But what?

"Shit, I gotta stop thinking about this," Jenny told herself while pacing an already worn out carpeted floor, after the last of three cigarettes smoldered in the ashtray. "And I have a story to write," she thought. "What the hell am I going to write about? Certainly not the truth. I'll end up right back in a mental institution."

"It has to end though," she continued moments later, turning the knob on the shower valve and testing the temperature with her finger. "Whatever happens, this is definitely the end and then I can get on with my life."

"Gas!" she exclaimed moments later, slipping into a worn out but comfortable pair of pajamas. If the game was the only way to open the gate, she would need gas for the generator, if it even still worked. That was a gamble, but a chance she would have to take. It would be impossible to power it up without electricity and she knew just who to call.

"Hey, this is Jenny Aldren," she said into her phone, while looking at the card she was holding in her hand. "I don't know if you remember me, but..." she began to say.

"Yeah, sure I remember you," the taxi cab driver answered after a brief pause. "You're the writer. I dropped you off at the Franklin mansion."

"Yes!" Jenny exclaimed. "So, I need your help."

"You need a ride?" he asked. "Sure, no problem. Where to?"

"Well, not tonight...tomorrow night, but the same place," she answered. "But I need you to do me a favor."

"Yeah...honestly I don't think I can help you with that," he replied.

"But why not?" she asked. "You told me to call you if I needed help."

"It will be Halloween night ma'am," he answered. "That's the last place I want to go to. Remember that picture you took for me?"

"Yes, of course," Jenny answered.

"Yeah well, there were some weird eyes staring out from the second story window," he stated. "So I ain't going near there, especially on Halloween."

"Please, I'll pay you double what your fare is," Jenny said.

"I don't know," he said, not sure but thinking about it.

"Look, I'll pay you two hundred dollars," Jenny offered. "That's more than you would make in an entire night."

"Two hundred you say?" he asked to make sure.

"Yes, but I need gas," she answered.

"Gas?" he returned bewildered. "What the hell do you need gas for?"

"For a generator," she said "A five gallon gas can filled would work."

"Well, I would have to buy one first of all," he replied. "I don't have gas cans lying around."

"Do you want to help me or should I call someone else?" she asked, losing her patience.

"Two hundred plus you pay for the gas and the damn can I gotta buy," he offered.

"Agreed," Jenny said. "Pick me up around 10:30."

19

RESURRECTION

"Balance of life restored,
The dead you shall be no more."

...*Hallows Eve*...

"Thanks so much," Jenny said, getting out of the cab, stuffing a flashlight in her back pocket, and reaching for her wallet while holding a small bag with the game and console inside. "I really do appreciate it."

"Yeah sure," he replied, stepping out himself. "Let me get your gas."

It was eleven o'clock at night and unlike five years ago, there was no moon in the sky. It was as dark as dark could be, making the cab driver feel even more uneasy than he already was. Jenny still had plenty of time, but certainly none to waste. Elizabeth would be here shortly, and she would have to make sure the game was ready to go to open the gateway. If the cab driver was nervous, it was no match for what she was feeling at the moment.

"Hey look," he said, pulling the gas can out of the trunk and closing it with a thud that sounded much louder than it would have been had it not been so quiet outside. "Just pay me my fare and for the gas and can."

"No, I promised you two hundred dollars," Jenny rebutted, reaching out her hand with the money.

"I can't take that much money," he refused. "Seriously, sixty dollars and fifteen for the gas and can. So, make it seventy-five."

"Are you sure?" Jenny asked.

"I'm sure," he replied. "I don't know why a woman like you would want to put electricity into that house, but you have more balls than me. So I guess it's the least I can do."

"You wouldn't believe me even if I told you," Jenny said, counting her money and handing it to him.

"It's eighty," she said as he took it. "I don't have change."

"Are you sure you want to do this?" he asked, stuffing the money in his pocket and handing her the gas can. "I mean, I can take you back right now…no charge. I'm going back in that direction anyway."

"No thanks…but yeah," she said. "I have to."

"Come here," he said walking to the front of the cab near the headlights. "Do you have a pen?"

"Actually I don't," Jenny said. "I'm really short on time."

"Alright wait a second," he said, going back to the cab and opening his door.

"I really have to go," Jenny reiterated, holding the can and the bag in her hands.

"Just one second," he stated, finding a pen in his glove compartment. "Well hell, I guess I'm just old school," he said, walking back to the front of the cab and headlight beams, to jot down a number on a business card. "That's my home phone. If you have any problems, you call me there. I mean…in case I'm done for the night."

"Alright, thanks," Jenny said, taking the card in her hand with the bag wrapped around her wrist.

"Be careful," he said, walking back to the car door.

The cab driver waited a minute as he watched Jenny from his headlight beams struggling to carry the gas can and bag while holding the flashlight at the same time. "I must be crazy," he thought to himself rolling down his car window. "Do you need some help?" he called out.

"It would be nice," she yelled back, setting the gas can down.

"I was afraid she would say that," he mumbled to himself, getting out of the car. "Here, I'll take the can and bag. You lead the way."

"Thanks again," Jenny said, pointing the flashlight ahead. "Watch your step. The weeds are pretty thick but there's kind of a path now."

"I'm not going in the house though," he said following behind her.

"No, you don't have to," she stated trudging forward. "The generator is in the back."

Jenny was trying not to think about it, but it was impossible. Five years ago today she was here with her friends. She could almost even see their faces. She could hear Brandon complaining about Mike and Tyler being so late and that there was no beer. Brian was talking about the latest software technology. Even the sound of the weeds brushing against her legs reminded her of that night. It seemed just like yesterday.

"Here it is," Jenny said, reaching the generator and the blue tarp draped over it.

"Jesus, how old is that thing?" the cab driver asked, after Jenny had removed the cover.

"It's a piece of shit. I know," she agreed.

"Alright, shine the light closer and we'll see if we can get it started," he said.

Jenny steadied the flashlight while the cab driver removed the gas tank cap and began filling it up.

"I don't know," he said, observing the generator closer as the gas can gurgled its liquid. "Even the spark plug looks corroded. That oughta about do it," he said a moment later, content that it was full. "Still got half a can left."

"So, do you think it will start?" Jenny asked.

"Well, let's find out," he said, giving a hard pull on the cable with no result. "I think the choke's stuck," he concluded after several more failed attempts.

"Great," Jenny said, beginning to think this whole thing was a bad idea.

"Just hold on," he said, fumbling with the choke and finally freeing it loose. "Now let's try it." The cab driver pulled once again on the cable, only this time it roared to life spitting and sputtering at first and then settling into a loud but steady rumble. "Looks like you got a light on in there," he noticed glancing over to the parlor door.

"Oh my God! Thank you so much," Jenny said, reaching over to hug him. "I don't know what I would have done without you."

"You're quite welcome Mrs. Aldren," he replied, hugging her back. "Now you be careful and like I said…call that number I gave you if it gets late and you need a ride or something."

"I will. And thanks again," she said smiling.

…Less than an hour later…

"Boo!" Elizabeth yelled, sneaking up from behind Jenny, as she was on her knees attaching wires to the game box.

"Jesus!" she yelled, jumping nearly two feet in the air and dropping the box. "You scared the shit out of me!" she continued, turning around to see Elizabeth standing there. "I didn't even hear you come in."

"I floated over," Elizabeth answered. "It's a joke," she added, seeing the bewildered look on Jenny's face.

"Funny," Jenny returned, not laughing. "I see you're dressed for the occasion," she said with sarcasm, noticing Elizabeth was wearing the same elaborate black outfit she had worn during the night of the game.

"You like?" Elizabeth asked, spinning around to model it.

"I mean if you like the gothic 18th century look," Jenny replied.

"I do actually," Elizabeth said. "You look…well…nice."

"Uh huh," Jenny said back, not interested in her fake compliment.

"You should do something with your hair though," she added, reaching out to touch it.

"Get off!" Jenny exclaimed, pushing Elizabeth's arm away.

"Well, I'm just saying," Elizabeth stated. "That time of the month?"

"I'm not here to be your friend or talk about fashion and hairstyles," Jenny made clear. "Okay?"

"Pity," Elizabeth said. "Let's have a look around, shall we?"

"We don't have much time," Jenny informed her.

"We have plenty of time, child," she disagreed. "Sorry," she corrected herself, seeing the angered expression on Jenny's face. "We have plenty of time, Jenny," she repeated. "Better?"

"I hate it when you call me that," Jenny informed her.

"Indeed," Elizabeth agreed.

"It's just that it's hard to look at you," Jenny said as they started to walk casually through the house side by side. "It's weird. I mean, I know you're not Dana, but…"

"I know," Elizabeth said. "You don't have to explain."

"It was wrong what you did to her," Jenny said after a moment of silence fell between them.

"Well, I'm here, aren't I?" Elizabeth stated with a question.

"And it was wrong what you did to my friends. And me," Jenny went on, but only this time there was no reply from Elizabeth. "What was it like living here?" Jenny asked, as they entered the kitchen and changing the subject. "I mean back then."

"Hello mother," Elizabeth said with little emotion.

"She's here?" Jenny asked.

"Yes, in this room," she answered. "I can feel her."

"Where is she?" Jenny asked.

"In her chair," Elizabeth said. "Over there," she pointed.

"Hi Mrs. Franklin," Jenny waved, feeling stupid.

"It was different," Elizabeth began to answer Jenny's question. "We didn't have phones or computers, of course. Or even cars for that matter. But we made do."

"Did you have those beautiful gowns you see women wearing in the movies?" Jenny asked.

"I thought we weren't talking about fashion," Elizabeth smiled, running her fingers across the dusty countertop. "Yes, of course I did. Several as a matter of fact."

"You must have felt like a Princess wearing them," Jenny smiled back and realizing there was more to Elizabeth than she had given her credit for.

"Well, it was common for a lady to look like that Jenny," she said. "Of course, I came from a rich family so my dresses were a bit more extravagant."

"I can imagine," Jenny agreed. "What about the war? I mean you were actually there. All we can do is read about it."

"Oh please, I wouldn't bore you with such talk about war," Elizabeth said.

"No, I want to know," Jenny said.

"Some other time," Elizabeth replied.

"Do you miss it?" Jenny asked. "Living back then?"

"I miss living," Elizabeth answered, looking at Jenny directly into her eyes.

"But not at the expense of someone else's life," Jenny said, with a lump in her throat.

"I'm here to fix that," Elizabeth said, turning away from eye contact. "I would say something but…"

"What?" Jenny asked. "Say it."

"For someone with no powers, you have been quite an adversary," Elizabeth finished. "I admire you for that."

"I don't want to be your adversary," Jenny said.

"Really?" Elizabeth asked. "I thought you enjoyed that."

"No," Jenny simply answered. "It's just...I mean... I understand you would want to come back...who wouldn't if there was a way to do it. But why did you have to kill my friends?"

"The game?" Elizabeth questioned, casually walking over to the fireplace where her mother had taught her how to cook.

"Yes," Jenny replied.

"I regret that," Elizabeth admitted, turning the rusted handle of the spit to see if it still worked. "But it was what I was told to do," she said looking over to Jenny. "I was in hell for 150 years. I had no idea about your world now. You can blame my grandmother for that I guess. She is the one who put the evil in my heart."

"I would like to believe that you regret it," Jenny said. "I really would, but I don't trust you."

"And you shouldn't," Elizabeth countered. "I'm a witch. Deception is our best ally. I have said this numerous times."

"So are you deceiving me now?" Jenny asked, touching Elizabeth's hand that was still resting on the crank of the spit and making eye contact.

"What does your heart tell you?" Elizabeth asked, staring back.

Jenny paused for a second trying to read Elizabeth's eyes for the truth, but it was impossible. She could only hope the feeling in her heart, as Elizabeth suggested, did not lie to her.

"Ugh!" Jenny conceded breaking eye contact with her.

"And?" Elizabeth asked.

"There are two sides of you, and I'm not sure which to believe!" Jenny exclaimed.

"Then pick one," Elizabeth suggested. "No?" she asked, noticing Jenny's silence after enough time had passed. "There are two sides to all of us Jenny," Elizabeth said, continuing through the kitchen and randomly touching things that to anyone else would seem trivial. "I'm certain there is a side of you that you are not particularly proud of," she surmised, looking over to Jenny still standing by the fireplace.

"Maybe," Jenny confessed but not willing to discuss it any further.

"See, you hide from it," Elizabeth pointed her finger at her to gesture. "And you shouldn't."

"Well nobody's perfect," Jenny countered.

"No, but what makes you weak can also make you stronger," Elizabeth preached.

"Yeah, I know the saying," Jenny agreed.

"So, embrace it," Elizabeth continued.

"It's hard to have a discussion like this with someone that wants to kill me," Jenny blurted out, surrendering her thoughts.

"Well, I'm not going to lie to you," Elizabeth admitted. "At one point I did."

"Did, as in past tense I hope," Jenny replied nervously.

"Yes, but not now," Elizabeth agreed.

"And why not?" Jenny asked, relieved but curious just the same.

"Would you rather it be the other way around?" Elizabeth countered with her own question, still preoccupied with surveying the room and looking up to the ceiling to notice the structural cracks that had begun to jeopardize its integrity.

"That's a dumb question…of course not," Jenny answered. "Planning to remodel or something?" she asked, annoyed that Elizabeth was so preoccupied.

"Maybe actually," Elizabeth agreed, lowering her eyesight down from the ceiling and back to Jenny to give her her full attention.

"I don't want to kill you, because in many ways you and I are the same," Elizabeth explained, walking back over to her. "This I have come to realize."

"You and I are definitely NOT the same," Jenny disagreed emphatically.

"Oh yes we are," Elizabeth countered back, leaning into her with those eyes that made Jenny feel uncomfortable. "We share the same destiny, you and I," she continued. "My grandmother would say that the future is difficult to predict, but yet I see it quite clearly."

"What do you see clearly?" Jenny asked with a shaken voice, backing up from her to gain some distance until her back was against the stone wall of the fireplace.

"You and I will be sisters," Elizabeth pronounced, inches from her face with eyes radiating with blue electrical charges.

"Please, you're scaring me," Jenny begged, turning her head away from her.

"That is not my intention," Elizabeth assured her, backing off to give her some space.

"Look, I'm not going to be your sister," Jenny said, trying to regain her composure and trembling. "I'm not a witch and even if I were..."

"You will be," Elizabeth interrupted to inform her.

"How do you know that?" Jenny demanded.

"I sensed it the moment we were alone in this house together," Elizabeth answered. "It speaks to me, especially here...in this kitchen."

"Well, I don't believe you," Jenny argued against the notion. "And besides...why did you bring that?!" Jenny exclaimed, noticing the handle of Elizabeth's dagger protruding out from Elizabeth's witches dress.

"It's not for you," Elizabeth answered, tucking it back away.

"For Dana?" Jenny asked.

"No!" Elizabeth replied.

"For who then?" Jenny asked once again.

Elizabeth had once again allowed her thoughts to become conflicted. Her vision of sisterhood with Jenny had taken her mind off of her objective. True, a part of her enjoyed Jenny's company, and she longed

199

for a friend. But it had made her weak, and that was not why she was here. She was here to kill the High Priestess, and Jenny as well.

"It is not of your concern!" Elizabeth exclaimed, as the fiery blue haze returned in her eyes. "We must begin. It is almost the Witching hour."

"So much for the tour then, right?" Jenny stated following Elizabeth, who had quickly left the room to head towards the parlor.

"Is the game in place?" Elizabeth asked, standing before it.

"Yeah, but I still have to make one more connection," she said, bending down to grab the wire.

"Then do it," Elizabeth said sternly.

"Hey, I'm not your slave Goddammit," Jenny said, turning around to address her as she plugged the last wire into the box. "That's it. We're good to go."

"Turn it on," Elizabeth said.

"You didn't say the magic word," Jenny teased.

"We do not have time to play games, child!" Elizabeth yelled, as the skeleton features of her face began to extrude from her skin.

"Shit, I guess you're right," Jenny agreed, seeing it and becoming unnerved. "It's on."

Elizabeth extended her hand out over the game apparatus, making it glow blue in an intensity that nearly matched the color of her concentrated eyes.

"What are you doing?" Jenny dared to question.

"Deleting its memory," Elizabeth offered, staring down at it. "That is, of course, unless you would prefer to play this game again?" she asked, turning her attention back to Jenny.

"Not funny," Jenny replied.

"Follow me," Elizabeth ordered.

It was odd, Jenny thought to herself following Elizabeth to the large cellar door and trying to keep up with her fast pace. How one moment she could almost pass for her best friend, and then in the next…a powerful and most vicious witch. She would have to be careful. There was no way she could trust her.

"This is the gateway you created," Elizabeth stated, opening the lock to the weapons depot as they arrived. "Do you remember it?"

"Yes, of course," Jenny replied.

"Stay close to me," Elizabeth said. "It will not go as easy as you think."

"Well, I never thought it would," she admitted, waiting to follow Elizabeth into the white room.

Elizabeth opened the door and entered the gateway as Jenny followed her. It was exactly as she had remembered it to be, white walls, white floors, white ceiling…just like the game, only devoid of creatures intent on killing you.

"Nobody's here," Jenny acknowledged, hearing her voice echo against the empty space.

"Any minute," Elizabeth said, standing her ground. That minute came and went.

"Well, maybe you can…" Jenny began.

"Quiet," Elizabeth interrupted her. "They're coming. I can feel it."

And then in an instant they appeared out of nowhere. Only it wasn't the High Priestess. It was Griselda, Queen of the Underworld, accompanied by the Four Gatekeepers. Dana was tightly in the grasp of the Elder and obviously under some sort of spell. She stood motionless, eyes closed and her head down.

"Griselda!" Elizabeth gasped in shock and dropped to one knee, bowing her head.

"Get on your knee Jenny," she whispered, looking over at her still standing.

"Fine," Jenny said, kneeling down. "But who the fuck is she?"

"She is Griselda," Elizabeth whispered from her bowed head. "Queen of the Underworld. Hades' wife."

"Shit," Jenny whispered back.

"Exactly," Elizabeth agreed.

"You were expecting someone else?" Griselda asked.

Griselda was actually quite tall, at least several inches more than Elizabeth…maybe taller given the black boots she was wearing. She stood in a black dress cut fairly low below her breasts and her raven colored hair (the same as Elizabeth's in length) was mostly covered by an ornate headdress. It was familiar to Elizabeth. The kind only someone with absolute power was allowed to wear, like horns turned upside down. She was holding a golden scepter in her hand that stood from the floor to well above her head in height, glowing in bright red at the top. Despite her daunting appearance, she was beautiful.

"I was actually," Elizabeth answered, still on one knee as was Jenny, and not looking up.

"You may rise," Griselda stated. "Is she the one?" she asked the younger of the gatekeepers as Elizabeth and Jenny stood.

"The smoker, yes," he answered with rolled back white eyes.

"Take her," Griselda ordered.

"Wait…what?" Jenny exclaimed, as two of the gatekeepers approached and grabbed her by the arms.

"Your gateway has caused quite a problem," Griselda said, as the guardians drug Jenny, despite her efforts to resist, next to the side of Griselda and opposite Dana. "I am here to see it never happens again."

"This is bullshit!" Jenny exclaimed. "I'm not part of your people and your fucked up world!"

"You have made yourself a part of it!" Griselda growled back.

"Get off of me you piece of shit!" Jenny yelled to the guardian holding her with one arm around her neck.

"Silence!" Griselda yelled. "I will not waste my energy on you, but you do test my patience!"

"Just relax Jenny," Elizabeth called to her.

"Ahh…" Griselda acknowledged. "So your grandmother was right. You have grown weak to the mortals."

"She would not have said that," Elizabeth stated.

"But indeed she has," Griselda shot back. "She has betrayed you."

"That is impossible," Elizabeth said with confidence.

"It is with your grandmother that I have made a deal," she returned. "So you see, you stand here before me in a most troublesome predicament."

"Forgive me Queen," Elizabeth said, trying to maintain her composure and respect, "but the deal was supposed to have been made by the High Priestess."

"And now the deal is being made by me," Griselda informed her.

"Then what is to become of me and my sister?" Elizabeth asked, folding her arms across her chest and shifting her weight.

"Hey, don't forget about me," Jenny jumped in, waving her hand in the air, devoid of any attention back.

"Dana will be spared," Griselda replied. "I will return her back to the living. It is the wish of your grandmother. The two of you she has no use for."

"But why?" Elizabeth asked. "Why does she request this? I don't believe you."

"Because YOU are reckless," she answered, raising her voice. "There are only two heirs left to the Franklin dynasty, you and Dana. Which begs the question," she said leaning on her scepter in Elizabeth's direction and staring into her eyes. "Why should you be given the opportunity to represent a legacy you have purposely tried to destroy?"

"I came here to correct that!" Elizabeth exclaimed, defending herself.

"Too little, too late," Griselda hissed. "No, you belong in hell with me, the moon daughter I intended you to be in the first place."

"She may be reckless, but she is my daughter," Mary Franklin said, materializing in human form in front of Elizabeth.

"Mother!" she exclaimed.

"Stay behind me Elizabeth," Mary ordered.

"How quaint," Griselda said. "To be willing to protect the very one that took your life and stole your powers."

"A mother's bond runs deep," Mary stated. "Spare her, I beg of you."

"The deal has already been made," Griselda said, lowering her scepter as it shot a bolt of red colored lightning out, crackling with energy as it split the air and disintegrated Mary in an instant.

"Damn you!" Elizabeth growled from now skeleton teeth and eyes of blue flames. Raising her hands, she released a stream of blue electricity so intense that it temporarily blinded Jenny and struck Griselda unexpectedly in the shoulder.

"Ahh!" she winced, instinctively reaching with her hand to her blackened and burnt skin and dropping the scepter.

"Oh this can't be good," Jenny said, trying to see.

"My powers are stronger than you think bitch," Elizabeth snarled, raising her hands and releasing her energy once again. This time she hit Griselda directly in the chest and knocked her off of her feet.

Jenny could smell burnt flesh and what reminded her of charred electrical wires permeating the air, as the guardian tightened his grip on her. Surprisingly, they stood their ground and did nothing to intervene in the battle taking place.

"How dare you strike me!" Griselda exclaimed, rising up on her feet and reaching out with her own hands in the same manner Elizabeth had.

But Elizabeth was ready for her and no sooner than Griselda had released her charge, she had done the same, as blue and red lightning met together and fizzled out harmlessly.

"Enough of this!" Griselda clenched her teeth, extending her arm and hand out while the scepter flew through the air off the floor and into her grasp and within seconds unleashed its fury.

This time Elizabeth was unprepared. The bolt of red energy struck her directly, knocking her to her knees. But rather than dissipating, the energy engulfed her almost like a sphere and grew in intensity. Jenny's eyesight returned and she could see the agonizing pain in Elizabeth's human state face trapped in Griselda's containment, while the bluish haze of her eyes faded rapidly.

"Elizabeth!" she cried out, watching while the electrical charges danced across Elizabeth's face and body. "Stop it, you're killing her!" Jenny screamed to Griselda.

"Precisely," she acknowledged smiling.

"And I've had about enough of you!" Jenny yelled, slamming the guardian with the back of her elbow into his face. The blow wasn't hard enough to do much damage but enough for him to momentarily lose his grip on her. That was all she needed, and she ran to Elizabeth's side.

"You can't help her fool," Griselda laughed, motioning for the guardian to stay put.

"Yeah, we'll see about that," Jenny replied, seeing the top of Elizabeth's dagger protruding from its hidden place beneath her clothes.

"Sisters," Jenny whispered to Elizabeth, winking as she reached through the electrical sphere and grabbed the handle.

"Yes," Elizabeth agreed, crying and knowing what she was about to do.

Jenny pulled the sacrificial dagger out, burning her hand in the process. She charged with all her might towards Griselda, catching her completely off guard. Before she could even react, Jenny raised the dagger in the air. Screaming with rage, she plunged it directly into Griselda's heart, lowering the sphere containing Elizabeth instantly.

"Nooo!" Elizabeth screamed, as Jenny pushed even harder on the dagger. Griselda's power began to run in the same manner Elizabeth's mothers had, through the dagger and into her. It was exhilarating but at the same time painful, and she felt like she was on fire.

"Jenny, let go!" Elizabeth screamed. "She's too powerful. It will kill you!"

"I'm trying!" Jenny yelled back. "I can't."

Elizabeth stumbled to her feet but collapsed instantly. She was too weak to walk.

"Dana! Sister!" Elizabeth screamed. "Wake up child, we need you!"

The guardians had left. More than likely to inform Hades, but regardless they were not warriors and were not permitted to intervene. That left Dana standing alone unrestrained but still in a coma state of mind, staring expressionless and oblivious to what was going on.

"Elizabeth please!" Jenny yelled, noticing her hand beginning to smolder. "I'm burning!"

"Dammit!" Elizabeth cursed, fighting the conflict in her mind as she stood on her hands and knees spitting up blood. "The vision must be true," she thought to herself. They were to be sisters. "I'm coming!" she yelled, mustering every ounce of energy she had and rising to her feet. She would not allow herself to be beaten, and she would not watch her new friend…her sister…die before her eyes. Willpower was all that afforded her now. Reaching Jenny as quickly as she could, Elizabeth placed her hand over hers and the handle of the dagger. She could not break the grip the energy had over Jenny, but she could at least partially absorb it. The power she felt flowing through her was enormous, and she wondered how Jenny was even still alive. Seconds felt like an eternity, while both she and Jenny's bodies convulsed uncontrollably. And then souls of thousands, in the shape of white orbs, began fleeing from Griselda's body, captive over centuries and disappearing from the room within seconds. Griselda's body split in half, revealing a blinding white light that shot straight up to the ceiling and then vanished. What remained of her turned to a pile of ash, leaving the dagger to fall from their hands to the floor with a loud metal clang in the suddenly quiet room. It was over.

"Jenny!" Dana exclaimed. The spell was broken, and she watched both Jenny and Elizabeth fall to the floor from exhaustion. "What the hell happened?" she asked, running over to them. "I was coming to the light when the gateway opened. I was coming through and then everything went black."

"Griselda put a spell on you," Elizabeth replied, lying flat on her back. "She and the four guardians followed you through."

"Oh that's not good!" Dana exclaimed.

"Relax," Jenny said, lying flat on her back as well, almost too tired to talk. "I killed her."

"You did what?!" Dana asked in disbelief. "You killed the Queen?"

"You don't have a cigarette, do you?" Jenny asked, staring up at the white ceiling.

"This isn't funny," Dana stated. "Do you have any idea what they will do to you? They're going to come for you…both of you…and me!"

"Yeah well…" Jenny began, pulling herself up from the floor and reaching out her hand to pull Elizabeth up as well. "She was going to kill us both. So better not to be dead, right?"

"And that's not funny either," Dana replied. "Am I missing something here?" she asked, noticing how Jenny and Elizabeth were standing next to each other, not as enemies but more like friends.

"Actually, yes," Jenny answered. "Just give me a minute."

"Oh my God, you have her eyes!" Dana exclaimed suddenly, noticing in shock.

"Really?" she asked, as Elizabeth turned to look at them and smiled.

"Indeed," she confirmed.

"You're a witch?" Dana asked.

"I don't know?" Jenny replied more like a question. "Elizabeth, am I a witch?"

"You are now," Elizabeth confirmed.

"I'm so confused," Dana admitted.

"And we are sisters," Elizabeth informed Dana.

"Yes, I know," Dana said.

"I'm sorry for what I did sister," Elizabeth offered. "I came here to rectify that mistake, but my grandmother deceived me."

"That mistake will still be rectified," came the voice of Mary Franklin, materializing once again into the room and accompanied by the High Priestess.

"Mother!" Elizabeth exclaimed. "You're alive!"

"Not in the manner of which you are, but in spirit…yes," Mary Franklin responded.

"Forgive me High Priestess," Elizabeth said, taking one knee to the floor.

"Oh…this again," Jenny said, doing the same and followed by Dana. "She's not going to try to kill us too, is she?"

"Shh!" Elizabeth whispered back.

"This gateway must be closed," the High Priestess said. "You are in grave danger, so we must make this quick."

"Yes, High Priestess," Elizabeth agreed.

"May I know your name please?" the High Priestess asked, looking over to Jenny.

"Jenny Aldren, ma'am," she replied.

"Jenny Aldren," she addressed. "You have killed the Queen of the Underworld. A most unwise thing to do."

"She was killing Elizabeth," Jenny stated.

"Do not interrupt me," the High Priestess noted. "I am aware of that. By virtue of her death, you and Elizabeth have inherited her powers. That makes me very nervous. Will you, Jenny Aldren, pronounce your faith to abide by and honor the Witches' Code?"

"I will," Jenny answered, swallowing hard and not believing what was happening or that she was even agreeing to it for that matter.

"Will you, without grievance in your heart, honor Elizabeth as your sister?" she asked.

"Yes, of course," Jenny answered, looking over at Elizabeth.

"The sacred dagger please," the High Priestess ordered.

Elizabeth rose to retrieve the dagger laying behind her on the floor and handed it, handle forward to the High Priestess.

"This is going to hurt a bit," Elizabeth whispered to Jenny, taking her place back on her knee beside her.

"Wait...what?" Jenny asked, not realizing what was coming.

"Hold out your hands please," the High Priestess said.

"Palm up," Elizabeth corrected Jenny, taking her hand by the wrist and turning it upwards.

"By the power bestowed upon me," the Priestess said, taking the dagger and slicing a deep cut across both of their palms. "I pronounce you sisters for eternity."

"Jesus!" Jenny exclaimed, seeing the blood gush out of her palm.

"Hold your hand out," Elizabeth told her.

"I got it," Jenny said, wrapping her fingers around Elizabeth's and sealing the bond with their blood.

"Sisters," Elizabeth said.

"Sisters," Jenny agreed.

"Dana Reynolds," the High Priestess called out. "You come from a very long line of Franklins."

"Yes, I am aware of that now," Dana acknowledged.

"Therefore, by virtue of your ancestry, the ritual of sisterhood is not necessary," she stated.

"I understand," Dana returned.

"But to walk amongst the living again, I must reverse that which Elizabeth has done," the High Priestess informed.

"Please, I beg you," Dana said.

"Rise sisters," she ordered. "Elizabeth, you continue to prove yourself as a most ambitious but troubling witch. In your short life, you have managed to circumvent the rules of which you are abided to, the sisterhood in which you are to consult with, and the code by which you are to follow. All, I might add, for personal gain and your quest for power and immortality."

"Forgive me, High Priestess," Elizabeth said solemnly.

"I think tolerate would be a word more well suited," she replied sternly. "There was no power greater than Griselda. Just because you have that power now, do not think you are entitled to privileges. The title of a High Priestess will be offered to you only after you prove to me that you are worthy of it."

"I understand," Elizabeth acknowledged, trying to control her emotions. She was not used to being talked to in such a manner.

"I don't want any more trouble from you Elizabeth," she warned. "I hope my words are clear."

"My allegiance is to you and the sisterhood," Elizabeth pledged.

"Perhaps," the High Priestess cautiously agreed, staring into Elizabeth's eyes trying to trust her. "We shall see."

"I will not fail you," Elizabeth reassured her.

"Very well then," the High Priestess concluded. "Bring in the body."

Immediately, two men in black hooded cloaks entered the room carrying the casket containing Elizabeth's body. You could not see their faces as they walked quietly and gently placed it on the floor in front of the High Priestess.

"Wait, where did that come from?" Jenny whispered to Elizabeth.

"When the four guardians came for Elizabeth to take her soul, the sisterhood arranged for a wall to be built in the cellar, from inside of which Elizabeth's body would be entombed," the High Priestess answered Jenny's question.

The two cloaked men then began to draw a large Pentagram across the floor and placed a single candle directly in the center, before taking their places on each end of the casket.

"I wonder what the candle is for?" Jenny thought to herself.

"It's to maintain balance within the life-force," Elizabeth answered her in her mind.

"You can read my mind?" Jenny asked, startled and looking over at her.

"Of course," Elizabeth said. "You can too. I just have to teach you."

"This is too weird," Jenny thought as Elizabeth smiled at her. "Alright, so I still don't understand though."

"To bring a life back from the dead, one must equally be taken. Like a trade," Elizabeth answered.

"So, someone...somewhere will die?" Jenny asked.

"Yes, but someone unworthy to live," Elizabeth replied. "The High Priestess will light the candle, and if it blows out then a trade has been made."

"We shall begin the ritual," the High Priestess announced, bringing flame to the candle by merely pointing at it. The two cloaked men then lifted the lid from the casket, as the smell of stagnated air and musty fabric escaped into the room.

"Oh, it smells awful," Jenny thought.

Time of over a century and a half had not been kind. The white dress Elizabeth's body had been dressed in was dry rotted and coming apart at the seams. Even the fabric the casket was lined with, once a majestic blue color, was pulling apart from the frame and blackened with mildew. All that remained of Elizabeth's body were bones. A single piece of jewelry, a silver necklace with a sapphire birthstone, was draped around her neck. It was the only thing that seemed alive.

"Your hand Elizabeth," the High Priestess commanded.

Elizabeth offered her the hand that had been cut and still bleeding. The High Priestess placed it over the gaping mouth of Elizabeth's skull and squeezed. Elizabeth winced from the pain, but she could not bear to look at her own skeleton body. She stood silent with her head turned as the blood trickled into the cavity of its jaw.

"That will do," the High Priestess said, releasing her hand. "Lay down child," she instructed her. "And Dana, you as well. Try to relax."

Elizabeth and Dana did as instructed and took their place next to the coffin of Elizabeth's true body.

"It is time," the High Priestess confirmed.

"Sisterhood of the 13 covens, harness the energy amongst you!" she began to recite. "And repeat my words."

"For thou whose spirit these bones now lay,

Heed this call…rise up and obey!

Follow through the mortal door,

Assemble flesh and walk once more.

Return these souls, I ask of thee,

Back to their bodies, so mote it be!"

Suddenly there came a gust of wind that instantly blew out the candle. Dana's soul began to fade away, leaving only her body that Elizabeth occupied laying on the floor.

"Dana!" Jenny yelled out, dropping to her knees next to her.

"Silence!" the High Priestess ordered with a gesture of her hand, standing over Elizabeth's coffin.

Jenny watched Dana's motionless face, waiting for some kind of sign…anything…but her eyes remained closed. She could hear (much to her discontent) the sounds of raw flesh growing and bones cracking, which went on for several minutes, almost making her nauseous. And then it stopped. Dana opened her eyes, seeing Jenny's own staring down at her.

"Jenny," she simply said.

"Welcome back," Jenny said, smiling and brushing Dana's hair from her face.

"Did it work? Am I alive?" Dana asked.

"Indeed," Jenny confirmed.

"Oh God, now you're even starting to sound like her," Dana said laughing.

"And Elizabeth?" Jenny asked, looking over at the High Priestess.

"See for yourself," she replied.

"Just relax for a minute," Jenny told Dana, getting up from her knees to walk over to the coffin.

"I can't believe it!" she gasped seconds later, looking in and seeing Elizabeth lying there staring up at the ceiling.

"And what is that which you can't believe?" Elizabeth asked, looking over smiling.

"How do you feel?" Jenny asked, knowing it was a rhetorical question.

"Alive!" she exclaimed. "But can someone please help me out of this dreadful box?"

Moments later with the aid of the two cloaked men, Jenny was standing side by side with the real Elizabeth Franklin...not from the spiritual world and not the spirit possessing Dana's body, but Elizabeth Franklin in the flesh. It took her a moment to take that all in and comprehend what had just happened.

"You're seriously going to need a new dress," Jenny joked, noticing the deteriorated fabric barely hanging onto her body.

"It's a pity," Elizabeth said observing it. "It was one of my favorites."

"Elizabeth!" Dana exclaimed, having stood up and approaching her to hug.

"I'm sorry," Elizabeth offered, hugging her back.

"Forget about it," Dana replied.

"Welcome back daughter," Mary Franklin said, admiring the friendship's Elizabeth had made and allowing them their time.

"Mother, most of all it is to you that I must apologize," she said, coming over to hug her as well.

"My only concern is your happiness and well-being," her mother returned, opening her arms to receive Elizabeth. "That is a mother's duty"

"Your love is truly unconditional," Elizabeth said, beginning to cry on her shoulder. "I should have realized that."

"And now you do," Mary said, placing a hand upon her head.

"There is a war coming," the High Priestess broke in. "Aurelia is next in line to the throne and will take her place beside Hades. She will come for all of you, perhaps even our sisterhood."

"We will be ready," Elizabeth declared, breaking the hug with her mother to address the High Priestess.

"Sisters of three," Dana said, raising her hand in the air while Jenny and Elizabeth joined in.

"Sisters of three!" they repeated in chorus, holding hands.

"Indeed," the High Priestess said, pleased to see. "And most powerful sisters you will be!"

The End

Coming soon...Sisters of Three

About the Author

Ronald George was born and raised in Maryland. He recently moved to the beautiful Florida gulf coast, where he enjoys being able to write outside year round in the beautiful sunshine. Ronald has always had an interest in writing and has been writing since he was a child. It is with great pride that he is finally able to share his creative skills with his first published novel in a three part series, Elizabeth Franklin: A Witch's Tale.

Printed in Great Britain
by Amazon